A New Moon Rises

Melody Greene

This book is a work of fiction. Names, places, characters and events are the product of the author's imagination or used fictitiously. Any similarities to actual events, places or persons, living or dead, are coincidental.

Copyright © 2017 by Melody Greene

No part of this work may be reproduced, stored in a retrieval system, or transmitted in any forms or means, without written permission from the publisher, except in the case of brief quotations embodied in critical articles or reviews. For information reach Black Print Publications Inc.

Black Print Publications Inc.
3916 Wahoo Dr. SE
St. Petersburg, FL 33705

www.blackprintpublications.com

First Edition: November 2017

Library of Congress Cataloging-in-Publication Data

Greene, Melody.

    A New Moon Rises / by Melody Greene. — 1st ed.
    p. cm.
    Summary: A shy but strong girl in Chile must face the legends of her father's stories to save her sister from a mystical fate.
    ISBN-13: 978-0-9991608-0-0 (pb)
1.   Juvenile Fiction. [1. Literature-Fiction. 2. Folklore-Fiction. 3. Fantasy. 4. Latin America-Fiction. 5. Family-Fiction 6. Friendship-Fiction.] I. Title.
 [Fic]

2017910015
10 9 8 7 6 5 4 3 2 1

Cover Art by Moreuvian and Seán-Lee

Illustrations and Book Design by Seán-Lee

Text was set in Century and Philosopher

Printed in the United States of America

For my mom,

who's supported every dream I've ever had.

Chapter One

As the sun set across the peaks of the Andes, the deepening rays cast an orange tint over the fields and mountains. This had always been Maritza's favorite part of the day. The dampness of churned soil mixed with hints of syrupy flowers drifted through the air. She closed her eyes and held out her arms as the scents of the field carried on the wind, and floated over her body.

It was the end of the day. She laid the last of her grapes into the wooden crate before

Papá lifted it with his strong arms. The sweet, dark berries overfilled the bulging crate. She dusted off her muddied knees and thumbed the golden ring on her necklace left behind by her Mamá. She thought back as she traced the grooves of the tiny rose engraved on its face.

Maritza didn't have many clear memories of Mamá, but she did remember her calling her "Zita." Only Mamá did this. And though she'd never admit it to anyone, it's what Maritza called herself in her deepest of hearts.

Running down the vineyard and dragging her cotton bunny, Conejito, behind her was Isidora, Maritza's little sister. Her lips were stained with purple grape juice from the handfuls of fruit she'd sneaked during the day, even though she knew she wasn't supposed to. And from the looks of it, Conejito had a few as well, though his floppy blue ears tried to hide the fact. Isidora wiped her mouth, leaving behind the giggling smile she always had. Maritza's mouth curved up in a twitch. As much as she loved her little sister, she was slightly envious of how happy she always appeared. People absolutely gravitated toward the little one.

Like her sister, Maritza had long, russet hair which seemed to glow red when reflecting the sun. They both had round almond eyes, but while Isidora's danced as though she were always at play, Maritza's brown eyes were piercing, as though she were always thinking about something. The villagers saw this in her and suspected she would be a very clever girl.

The girls followed Papá to the front gate where he helped load the last of the crates to be taken into the city. Papá lifted Isidora high into the air. The sweet girl chuckled as she pretended to be an airplane. Maritza laughed along as she remembered how Papá used to do the same for her when she was smaller. When her hair flung around and the world spun about her, she'd thought Papá was the tallest man in the world, but now that she was eleven-years-old she knew he was pretty average. His dark beard grew in patches, and he had a pot belly, but he was handsome to Maritza.

After the small delight, they all piled into the truck that would drive them back home for the night, to Santa Alma. The truck bumped along the rocky road climbing steeper into the mountains. Maritza and Isidora chattered and played, tossing Conejito back and forth.

"You know what tonight is, right?" Maritza said as she held the stuffed bunny out of Isidora's grasp.

"Yes!" Isidora howled. Her voice rang out like a schoolyard song. "Papá is going to tell one of his legends tonight! I can't wait for the fire! We can stay up extra late!"

Maritza scooted close to her little sister. "I know. It's going to be fun. He'll definitely tell the one about the boy in the well. I like the sound Papá makes when he pretends the boy is trying to climb out!"

"No! That one's too scary!" wailed Isidora. "He'll tell the one about the princess who became a tree."

"Well they're supposed to be scary," Maritza replied tapping Isidora on her forehead. "How about the one where the jaguar swallows the ruby, and is trapped in the temple as punishment?"

"Don't worry girls. I think I have something

you'll both like tonight," Papá chimed in. He widened his eyes and grinned. "A tale of treasure, of greed, and of course..." He drew his hands up like claws, "danger."

The girls stared with their jaws dropped and squealed in delight as the truck finally came to a halt. They darted out of the truck bed and into their two room house.

The house was made of adobe, coated with faded yellow paint, a thatched roof, and a wooden door that didn't quite reach the floor. Maritza skipped by the stone chimney and three rolled mats on which they slept and dragged her hand across their little wooden table. In the back room, Abuela could be heard snoring and occasionally shooing off a suitor in her dreamland. Maritza looked in on her, wanting her to hear Papá's story.

"Abuela, Abuela, wake up!" Maritza begged as she poked at Abuela's arm.

"Ay, Ramon, I told you the gazebo was the last time," Abuela muttered.

After realizing there was no waking her, Maritza grabbed Papá's *chamanto* he wore on special nights, and left to join everyone around the fire in the village center.

Papá took the *chamanto* from Maritza, patted her on the head, and pulled it down over his shirt. The red wool was embroidered with silken wheat ears and bellflowers. The silk threads shone brighter than ever in the light as the flames danced and licked at the stars and waning moon. Maritza and Isidora squeezed between some of the other children around the fire, and the villagers waited in awe for Papá to begin his tale. He took his place and blew into his wooden pan flute.

> *"Through all my years, I can still remember the stories my Abuelo used to tell me of his work in the mines. One always stuck out more than the others. He told me that while usually the miners were prosperous and found more than enough gold to keep their families fed and clothed, there were months where not a single nugget could be found in the mines. In these times people panicked, worrying about where their next meal would come from, or if they would have*

to abandon their homes to find new places to live. But then suddenly, as if by magic, the mines would begin to produce gold again. And the people would be happy.

For years the villagers went on like this, never questioning the sudden disappearance of the gold. However, my Abuelo hated the hard times and wanted to put a stop to them. So, the next time he saw that less gold was being dug up in the mines, he camped out above the entrance every night, in hopes of catching the thief.

One night under the waning moon, just like tonight, my Abuelo was dozing off as he overlooked the mines from a dry, grassy hill. The night was warm and heavy, and after a day of work, he wanted to rest his bones and sleep. Just as he was about to drift off to the land of dreams, he felt a great gust of wind at his back. Startled, he shot up and turned around as a shadow flew above him, darkening the sky. He rubbed his eyes in disbelief and looked to the mines just in time to see a golden feathered tail disappear into the darkness.

My Abuelo couldn't believe what he was seeing and pinched both of his cheeks to make sure he was awake. With uncertainty, he lit his lantern and climbed down the hill and into the mines. Going into the mines at night was dangerous, but he had to discover the truth. As he made his way inside, he could smell the warm night air mixing with the dust from carved out rocks. He felt his way down the caverns to the deepest part of the mine and there it was. A grand and magnificent bird of gold was hunched over, pecking at the shining flecks in the mine walls. Each time it found one, it would swallow the nugget and dig deeper and deeper looking for the next.

'So this is where the gold is going,' my Abuelo realized, 'right into this beast's belly!'

My Abuelo needed a plan. By the gold

of its feathers, and the way it devoured nugget after nugget, he knew this giant creature was none other than the Alicanto! It is said that the Alicanto is obsessed with and loves to eat gold. If you find it, sing its song, and it'll lead you to the greatest treasure of all. It goes like this:

> *Canto, hear my cry*
> *I need food for baby and I*
> *Your nest is full*
> *With all the jewels*
> *Give me some if I bow to you*

But, my Abuelo wasn't interested in treasure. He wanted the people of the village to be able to work and be happy with their families. So he left the mine to put his plan in motion. Everyone knows of our precious cornucopia. Years ago, it was formed from the melted gold of the mines to represent the continued abundance of grapes grown in our vineyards. The next morning my Abuelo went to the village Elder and insisted that he be allowed to use the cornucopia. After some pestering, the Elder finally agreed. Abuelo set up the rest of his scheme, and by nightfall he was on the hill waiting for the Alicanto to appear.

When the Alicanto came, my Abuelo took the cornucopia and followed it inside the mines. As Abuelo trailed closely behind, he stumbled over a rock, which made an awful noise. So awful the Alicanto turned and shone its golden eye. The light was so bright Abuelo shielded his sight before raising the cornucopia to lure the beast. The Alicanto ran towards Abuelo to claim his treat, and Abuelo bolted from the mine and up into the mountains. He ran true, even as he felt the rumble of the earth as the Alicanto gained closer to him. Finally, he reached a dark cave with a narrow opening. He jumped in, careful not to smash his lantern. The Alicanto snapped its sharp beak in the cave as it squeezed its large body through. Abuelo shook the cornucopia, and one hundred gold coins spilled into the back of the cave. Abuelo forgotten, the Alicanto flitted over him and pecked at the glimmering coins. While it was distracted, Abuelo picked up the chains he'd nailed into the walls during the day and snapped a shackle around each of the bird's legs. Quietly, he collected the cornucopia, and backed out of the cave. With all his strength he pushed two boulders over the opening of the cave. The rocks were so massive Abuelo could only move them a bit, but it was enough to seal the thieving bird.

Since then, no one has seen the Alicanto. The mines have remained prosperous, and our village has been happy."

Papá played a chipper tune on the pan flute, with resounding pitches from high to low. Everyone cheered and applauded as he showed his gratitude with a deep bow.

Soon after, the villagers dispersed from around the fire to retire to their homes.

Maritza and Isidora were right at Papá's heels, laughing and prodding him with questions to continue the story.

Back in the yellow house, after Isidora had been tucked in with Conejito snug in her tiny arms, Papá bent down to kiss Maritza goodnight. She was sleepy-headed and on the verge of slumber, but could still make out the fine creases in his deeply tanned face. Papá had puffy cheeks and always smiled, just like Isidora.

"Papá, did you ever see the Alicanto?" She asked.

"No I didn't *mi tesoro*. I was not yet born when Abuelo trapped it," Papá answered.

"Oh, it's just a story anyway," Maritza said with a yawn.

"What? No way, all of my stories are true!"

"Every one?"

"Every single one."

And with that, Maritza closed her eyes.

Chapter Two

The village center was busier than normal. Maritza always thought it seemed empty in contrast to the cities closer to the foothills. The ground was dusty and unpaved. Maritza stood in the cool shade offered by the only sign in the village, it read:

"Santa Alma
Grace be with Thee"

She looked around at the three vendors who came twice a week selling goods from the backs of their trucks. One brought chickens and eggs, one had ears of corn, and one sold grapes, possibly the ones she'd picked herself.

The vineyard was closed for the day and everyone was enjoying the time off. Kids played around the remnants of the bonfire. Isidora smiled proudly as she showed off Conejito to a boy with a tousled mess of hair. Some of the older men had set up a card table and were shouting over a game of dominoes. Papá had joined them and was tossing in a few coins for a bet. He loved dominoes and poker, even though he had a terrible poker face. Papá could never hide when he had a good hand. He always raised his left eyebrow and everyone knew it. But he always played because he enjoyed the company of his comrades. *Isidora really takes after him,* Maritza thought as she looked on, wishing she could do the same.

Maritza felt a tickle at the back of her neck and slapped her hand against it, thinking it was a bug. She turned around to two little girls dressed in matching red striped shirts and matching faces. She'd seen the twin girls around many times, as she'd seen most everyone, but she'd never spoken to them. They were giggling and blowing soapy bubbles from a wand. Their cheeks were rosy and their hair curled just beneath their ears. They seemed to be only slightly older than Isidora's own six years.

"Hello," said the girl on the left with a guffaw. "Do you want to play with us?"

"It's fun. Mommy bought these bubbles in town. See?" said the other.

The girls blew their bubbles again in a stream and one popped on Maritza's nose. The flying soap stung her eyes and she backed away from the girls as she desperately tried to rub away the burn.

"Sorry, but no thanks," Maritza answered.

"You're no fun," said one of the girls.

"Yeah big kids are mean," said her sister.

The twin girls skipped away, blowing bubbles and laughing over their precious toy. Maritza drooped her shoulders as she realized that she was alone. Again. Everyone in Santa Alma was running around and chatting while she stood beneath a post by herself.

Maritza jumped when a hand came down on her shoulder. She looked up and Papá was standing over her, smiling like always. He squeezed her slightly with his calloused hand as he turned her towards him.

"What was that about?" Papá asked, caressing Maritza's hair. "Your eyes are all red."

"It's nothing Papá," she answered. "They just wanted to play."

"Are you finished already? What was the game?"

"I...didn't want to play. They had bubbles and it stings."

"Would you have played if it was something other than bubbles?"

Maritza didn't answer. She kicked the gravel covering the ground around her shadow.

"Mari," Papá continued, "You should try more. Having friends is good, even if for a little while. I get worried about you. Look at Isidora over there having fun. I want to see that look on your face." He tilted up her chin towards him.

Isidora and the little boy had taken charred sticks from the night's fire. They shouted as they chased each other about, pretending to have a sword fight.

"Don't worry I'm okay," Maritza said as she turned away. "I have you and Isidora. Even Abuela is fun."

"There are a lot of people in the world Mari. And sometimes, we lose our loved ones."

Papá pulled Mamá's ring from beneath Maritza's collar and sat down leaning against the post.

"Mamá and I were childhood friends," he said. "When she was little, she was like you. She thought she liked to be by herself, and I would tease her by pulling her hair and drawing pictures on her desk. I know, I was a little mean. She didn't like me at first, but after a while she came around and soon we were thicker than honey. Just like the color of her eyes."

Maritza was taken aback. She'd never known she had something in common with Mamá. Papá didn't talk about her much, unless he was being very serious. She crouched down next to him. She wanted to hear more about the woman she'd barely gotten to know.

"I bought that ring with the savings from my first job. It wasn't much but she loved it. It was a long time coming, and in return she gave me the greatest gifts I could ever hope for, our family." Papá nearly choked on the words.

"Why did you do all that stuff if you wanted to be her friend?" Maritza asked.

"Oh, I don't know. I was just a silly boy then."

"You said she didn't have many friends either?"

"Not that I can think of. She sat alone, ate alone. Until, she decided to give me a chance. She made many friends after that. Those ties were very important to her and I want you to have the same. You're the best big sister Isidora could ever have, but you have to take care of yourself too. Understand?"

Maybe it's easy for him, but not for me. Opening up to anyone other than Isidora was frightening. What if they thought she truly was as weird as she felt? She didn't have anything interesting to talk about other than her few faded comic books and Abuela's silly dreams. Maritza turned Papá's words over in her head. She didn't want to disappoint him. There were many children in Santa Alma, surely there was someone she could give a chance to.

"Yes Papá," she said.

Papá rose above her once more and patted Maritza on her head. His eyes were full of worry and love as he messed her silky hair before going back to the card table. Maritza searched around the square, but everyone was still occupied. She fell back against the sign post with a grunt. She looked up to the empty sky, the red sun baking her skin.

So Mamá had trouble making friends too. Knowing they shared the same trouble made Maritza feel closer to Mamá, but she didn't feel any more open to making other friends. She still didn't know how to.

The other children were interesting, and liked to do a lot of different things. Some liked to play sports, or sing. Some went on trips and had stories to tell about where they'd visited. One girl had even moved away to California and never came back.

Maritza didn't feel like she had anything to offer a friend. She felt completely boring.

Maritza dug her hands into the dirt and squeezed the clay in her palms.

It's hopeless.

Chapter Three

Maritza woke up to the smell of fresh baked bread and sliced avocado. Beneath that, she recognized the faint, but familiar scent of sage. Abuela burned the dry, brittle leaves every morning to ward off bad spirits, or so she said. Abuela was setting breakfast on the table, and Isidora was bouncing on her little stool. Maritza sat down to the table, and squinted at the sunlight jutting harshly through the window. She knew it was well into the morning, and that they should have been at the vineyard by then.

"Abuela, where is Papá?" she asked.

"He said we could stay home today and play!" Isidora chimed in.

"Yes he said you girls go down there way too often with him, and that you need to make some new friends," said Abuela. As she sat down, her periwinkle mumu stretched over her gut. "Eat your breakfast, and go outside. Find a ball or something. Have fun."

Abuela reached over to her radio, and turned on her favorite novella *The Heart Never Dies*. Maritza always wondered why Abuela was so excited about the faceless voices that were always in dramatic fiascoes. It all seemed too silly and impossible to her. The girls hastily devoured their meal. Maritza sneaked an extra bit of bread into her coat pocket, and they were swiftly out of the door. They didn't even find out if the program's missing hero, Carlos, had really survived the shipwreck.

* * *

Maritza found her quiet spot beneath the village sign. She'd made a blunder of the day before, but she'd promised Papá she would try to do better.

Off to the side she spotted Isidora tossing pebbles in a game of hopscotch with a group of little girls her own age. Isidora was able to make friends with anyone. She would simply beam up at them with her round, smiling face. Once they saw how cheerful and cute she was, like she could do no wrong, they were in her palms. Maritza, on the other hand, was well aware she had a bit more trouble. As warm and engaging as her own eyes were, she was quite distant around new people. Most of the townspeople saw how shy she was, and kept away. It didn't help that she more than preferred to keep to herself. She knew what Papá really meant was that *she* was the one who needed to make more friends. She spotted another group of older girls playing jump rope near a barren tree. With a sigh, Maritza tucked Mamá's ring beneath her shirt and headed in their direction.

> *"School, school, the golden rule*
> *Pencil, paper, sign your name*
> *P-A-U-L-A"*

"Um, excuse me" Maritza interrupted.

"Do you want to try?" the jumping girl offered, while continuing to bound over the quickly turning rope. Her raven curls floated in the air as she descended to the dirt. Maritza knew this girl from school, Paula.

The girls stopped turning the rope to let Maritza in for a turn. Paula stepped aside, forming her cool eyes into narrow slits. They began the rhyme again.

> *"School, school, the golden rule*
> *Pencil, paper, sign your name..."*

In the tiniest voice, one only a bat could hear, Maritza began to spell her name.

"m-a-r..." she squeaked.

"We can't hear you!" came Paula's voice brimming with confidence. "If you aren't going to sing it right, then step out of line!"

Maritza's sharp cheeks immediately flushed

a near crimson red as the girls laughed around her. She knew this was a bad idea.

"Hello?" Paula said with sarcasm as she cupped her ear. "I guess she must've swallowed her own tongue for breakfast!"

The girls burst into a fresh roar of laughter. Paula stood tall over Maritza with the sun at her back. Her fists dug into her waist, and a thin smirk spread across her face. The other girls closed in behind Paula, and the panic Maritza felt turned into a twitch growing in her fingertips. *Definitely a bad idea. I was doing just fine alone.*

Maritza couldn't take another moment of embarrassment, and unable to come up with a response, she walked away willing herself not to run. Feeling the burn of the girls' stares piercing into her back, she abandoned her resolve and sprinted to the far edge of the village. She knew children weren't supposed to go out of Santa Alma this way. The roads were rocky, and there were rumors of a cougar on the prowl. But Maritza didn't care about this. She just had to get away. She needed to be alone.

Isidora saw her big sister running and covering her face, and rushed to follow behind her. By the time Isidora caught up to Maritza, they were walking up a steep, narrow path higher into the mountains.

"I'm sorry, don't worry about what happened back there," Maritza said without looking back.

"It's okay, I'll play with you. You're my favorite sister!" cheered Isidora.

"I'm your only sister, silly," Maritza said with a chuckle. "What about those girls you were playing with? Don't you want to stay with them?"

"No, it's okay. I just met them. I'll play with someone else tomorrow."

"I don't get it. How do you make so many friends?"

"It's so easy. I just walk up, and I say 'I'm Isidora, and I'm your friend now,' and then we play."

Maritza couldn't help but laugh. "Maybe I'll try it some time."

"What do you want to play?"

It always baffled Maritza how Isidora could

throw any troubles behind her, and put on a happy face. She was always ready to have fun, to brighten any mood. The little girl didn't quite understand how someone could feel so sad when she always felt so happy. Maritza never knew whether to bonk Isidora on the head, or scoop her up into her arms. She knew her sister only wanted to cheer her up, and that was good enough for now.

"Hmm, I think I want to play 'Monster'!" Maritza called.

Isidora screamed, and ran up the path as Maritza crossed her eyes, and stuck out her tongue. Maritza chased Isidora up the dirt road in their game of pretend. Isidora's hair whipped around her face as she looked back to see if Maritza was closing in on her.

"I'm going to eat you nom nom nom!" Maritza cried to the squealing girl.

They ran for a short time with Maritza letting Isidora stay a few feet in front of her. She always let her sister win at these kiddy games. Jealousies aside, she loved putting a smile on her sister's face, even when she was the one who needed to cheer up.

Further up the path the earth began to flatten out, and they came to a fork in the road. The girls knew the path to the right led down the mountain and to the town of Mijas, but they'd never gone to the left. Isidora grinned, signaling that she was ready for a new game, and skipped up the unexplored road. For the most part it looked like any other rocky road. The rocks cast different shades of gray on one another depending on the shadow they gave off. The girls climbed higher until they came to a cave with a narrow passage. It was carved right into the stone of the mountain. Two gigantic boulders bordered the cave entrance.

"Mari, Mari look! It's just like in the story!" cried Isidora as she darted ahead.

"Yeah, it does look like Papá's story," said Maritza as she shrugged and went over.

"How fun would it be to find the Alicanto's treasure? Let's try, you remember the song right?"

The air was cool and thin that high up in the mountains. The breeze blew steady as the girls peered through the set of rough boulders at the cave mouth, and began to sing.

> *"Canto, hear my cry*
> *I need food for baby and I*
> *Your nest is full*
> *With all the jewels*
> *Give me some if I bow to you"*

The girls laughed at the creepy superstition of such a song. Crickets chirped along, as though providing a back-up chorus. As they giggled and hummed the tune again, a most curious thing happened. A heavy flap sounded from within, and a strong stream of wind blew out of the cave, tousling their hair and nearly knocking them over. When the warm air hit Maritza's face, she wasted no time turning to run, but Isidora was more adventurous, and had already begun to slip past the boulders into the cave.

Maritza grunted in frustration knowing she couldn't leave her little sister behind, and pushed her way through. Besides, it was probably just a breeze coming from another exit in the cave. Isidora's small frame allowed her easy access, but Maritza had to squeeze herself in, and hold her breath to fit through the rocks.

"The treasure is here. I just know it!" Isidora's voice echoed in the cave.

Finally through, Maritza looked around the cave. It was much deeper than she first suspected. The only light was from outside, but it didn't reach too much farther than the entrance. The air was chilly and damp. Maritza heard drops of water falling into puddles on the cave floor. She rubbed her arms to gain some warmth. The pitter patter of Isidora's feet didn't help the eerie feeling as she ran around looking for the fictitious pile of gold.

"Isi, I don't like this, we shouldn't be in here."

"I'm sure it's here. Please, just let me look for one little minute? You can even count!"

"One minute, and I will count. One, two, three..."

"Wait wait wait! I'm not ready to start yet!" Isidora said in protest, though she was already rummaging in a corner.

Maritza, walked deeper into the cave occasionally turning over a slab here and there, but mostly just humoring Isidora. The longer she was inside, the better her vision adjusted to the dim lighting. Maritza could make out the high stone arches of the cave. When she squinted she could even see the shapes of hanging stalactites. Apparently, Isidora had adjusted as well for at that moment she called out.

"Mari, look I found it!"

However, Maritza's sights were trained on something else altogether. At the back of the cave she spotted a large rounded shadow. She tilted her head to make sense of the shape which seemed to be pulsing up and down as though it were breathing. Her own breath quickened, and she wrung her hands. She took a step back remembering what Papá told her the other night, *"...all of my stories are true! Every single one."*

Maritza's heart stopped in realization. *The Alicanto!*

"Isidora!" Maritza screamed.

But it was too late. As the Alicanto's golden eye opened, raining radiance throughout the cavern, Maritza turned just in time to see Isidora bent over smiling at a golden feather.

Maritza sprinted towards her. Time seemed to slow as Maritza pumped her arms and legs. Isidora giggling at her discovery was all Maritza could hear. And as Isidora grabbed the shining plume, it burst into a million specks of glittering dust, and covered the girl from head to toe. Isidora slumped over, and Maritza's knees slammed onto the hard cave floor as she dropped to catch her. Maritza shook her sister's shoulders frantically as she called her name, but Isidora would not be roused.

Chapter Four

"Isi, Isidora!" Maritza shook her sister, but it was in vain. Maritza knelt in close to look at her sister's little body. Lingering golden dust was nestled in the crevices of her closed eyes. Her arms lay limp at her side but she was still breathing. Maritza sighed in relief, but she knew her troubles were just beginning. She felt a growing rumble in the cave floor. Remembering the Alicanto she looked back to see it batting its yellow wings and stepping down from the pedestal. It wasn't how she imagined. Its legs were wobbly and scrawny, not helped by the weight of the rusted chains holding it captive. The golden feathers on its body were molting and did not glow with the radiance mentioned in Papá's story. Maybe after years of solitude, it'd grown weaker.

 A pang of pity for the beast rushed through Maritza, but not for long, for the Alicanto let out a ringing screech before it stormed towards the girls. Maritza tried to lift Isidora over her shoulder, but her body felt much heavier in the limp state. The bird was getting closer and Maritza grabbed the collar of Isidora's dress and dragged her towards the entrance just out of the Alicanto's reach. The bird shrieked and snapped at the girls, wanting its prey. Maritza panicked, pressing her nails to her palms, knowing she'd have to squeeze both herself and her sister out of the cave. With the Alicanto stomping and making a fuss, rocks fell and broke apart around them and she knew she didn't have much time. The chains might not hold forever.

A pointed sharp stalactite plummeted into the ground only a foot away from them and Maritza let out the scream that'd been building inside of her.

Not wanting to risk Isidora being trapped, Maritza decided to try to push the unconscious girl through the narrow passage first. She crossed her legs and pushed on her shoulders, with every inch, she could feel the Alicanto at her neck getting closer and more desperate.

One of Isidora's dusty black shoes got wedged beneath a rock. Maritza pushed her forward, but Isidora didn't budge. Maritza didn't want to go ahead and leave her sister exposed, but she knew she had to make a move.

She climbed over Isidora, trying to block out the snapping of the bird's beak and sucked herself in, holding her heavy breath, to pass through the rocks. She felt suffocated as she pressed between the boulders. Every second was so slow it was like running through water, but she broke free into the sunlight and dropped to retrieve Isidora. She pulled and wiggled the little shoe but it would not budge. Inside the cave she heard the sounds of the crashing stones and she pulled more vigorously.

Tears welled up in her eyes at the thought of not being able to free her sister. Of that monster eating her like a golden nugget. She yanked at Isidora's leg and her foot came loose from the stuck shoe. Maritza pulled Isidora the rest of the way by her feet and when the girl was finally free, she showered her dirty face with kisses. She looked at the little flecks of gold tinting Isidora's fingertips and pulled her up onto her back. She wept as she carried her sister down the path and towards home, with the Alicanto's cries threatening to drown out her own.

* * *

By the time Maritza made it to the edge of Santa Alma, she was panting and drenched with sweat. Her legs burned from the weight of carrying Isidora steadily down the mountain. She'd never known how strong she could be until it was her only choice. She willed her aching muscles into town.

She gently lay Isidora down and ran for help. It was mid-afternoon and the vendors from the city were finished packing up their trucks and driving to their own homes. Not many people were out and about, they were probably taking a siesta. Maritza found a familiar man who had a thick mustache and sometimes brought comic books and sour candies to the village.

"Señor, please help me," Maritza gasped between words. "There's something wrong with my sister, we were playing in a cave!"

Maritza left out the encounter with the Alicanto. She didn't want this man to think she'd gone mad. She led him back to where Isidora lay and he put his head to her chest.

"I believe she's just sleeping. What happened?" he said.

"She...slipped on a rock." Maritza knew she shouldn't lie, but now that she was safe she was beginning to question the whole event herself. But she'd have to worry about that later.

"Show me where you live" the man said as he gathered Isidora in his arms.

With the little yellow house in sight Maritza sprinted down the path. When she swung open the door Abuela was just where they left her staring intently at the radio.

"Ah girls, Carlos made it!" Abuela didn't even look up, "He was on a deserted island for five years and now he's home but Adrianna..."

Abuela forgot about her novella as the mustached man carried in her granddaughter and laid her on one of the straw mats. Abuela was speechless, but at this point Maritza couldn't hold her tongue any longer and the story burst out of her, along with a new stream of tears.

She rambled about the Papá's tale, about the jump rope and leaving the village, about looking for treasure even though it was dangerous and about escaping the Alicanto, apologizing the whole way through. When she was finished and out of breath the mustached man's eyes were larger than a bowl of soup.

"This sounds like a family issue," he said before slipping out of the door.

After the door closed Maritza braced herself and waited for the sharp words Abuela was surely going to yell at her. However, Abuela just knelt beside Isidora and brushed the hairs from her forehead. Her eyes trailed down to Isidora's doll-like hands. When she saw the now golden fingers she sprang into action. She went into the back room and began sifting through an old trunk. Maritza followed and peered at the dark leather with brass buckles and wondered what Abuela could want with a trunk at a time like this.

"Abuela, what are you doing?! We have to find Papá," she begged.

"Your Papá is too far away at work and won't be back for a few days." Abuela answered "You have to get going."

"Going? Going where?" Maritza wished Abuela would listen "We have to get to the village phone."

"Isidora is in a deep sleep and she's turning to gold. If you don't save her, we'll lose her forever."

Abuela finally found what she was looking for and rose to her feet with a colorful rope with five thick knots. The cord was braided with strands of green, red, yellow, blue, and purple.

"No, she just touched a feather." Maritza shook her head. "She'll wake up in the morning."

"Mari, you have to be brave." Abuela shoved the rope in Maritza's hands.

"What is this?"

"It's a quipu and it will help you on your journey. Our ancestors used them for hundreds of years to keep count of things. People, crops, time, anything. But this one is special. It has been in our family for generations. My mother gave it to me, and her mother before her, and so on."

"What? Why? How can a piece of rope help Isi?" asked Maritza, her heart was racing.

"I know it's difficult to understand. When I was a little girl, my mother told me that this quipu, the one that I pass to you, would help us in great times of need. I've never seen it used, but it will open your heart."

Cool air blew through the only window of the house, it seemed strange to Maritza that such wild things were happening on such a lovely day. It was as though if she could go outside to smell the wildflowers, everything else would be forgotten. Abuela pulled open a sack and began packing items into it. She packed a canteen filled with water, a loaf of bread, a bunch of grapes, a candle with matches, and Papá's *chamanto*.

"Where are we going?" Maritza was filled with anxiety.

"Not 'we' Mari, 'you'" Abuela said. "You need to go get some things and bring them back. Only a special remedy will wake Isidora. My mother told me about it. To get what we need won't be easy. She said to make the remedy you must become your true self."

"My true self? I'm just Maritza."

"No honey, you're more than just a name. I believe in you."

"What are you talking about Abuela? The only thing we need to do is find Papá. This isn't one of your novellas!"

"Maritza that's enough!" Abuela grabbed

Maritza's cheeks. "You will go, there isn't time. I will watch Isidora and get a hold of Papá."

Maritza was so overwhelmed with the events of the day. She felt as though one wave after another was crashing over her. She looked at Isidora on the mat, breathing but not moving. She sat beside her and felt the warmth of her cheeks. As she bent down to kiss Isidora's brow, she'd made her decision.

"What will I need?" she said.

Chapter Five

"The Río Serrano will be your guide," Abuela began. "It is said that the river leads those who are ready to a new life."

"A new life? Abuela it's a river it only goes one way," Maritza protested.

"Ay, you kids today have no imagination. These oral traditions have been passed down for years. Before you all were so concerned with superheroes and movies, kids heeded the warnings of elders," Abuela said. "Your Papá didn't believe me either, he told the stories for fun and now look!"

Maritza squeezed Isidora's hardened hand, wrapping her mind around what may be in store for her.

"You need to have faith," Abuela continued. "Now listen closely, you'll need five special ingredients to make the remedy. Start by going through Mijas."

Maritza's heart skipped a beat at the thought of going back up the mountain the Alicanto called home. But, knowing she had no other choice, she simply nodded her head in agreement.

"If you follow the path out of the town and along the river you will find an abandoned well. The well has been there as long as anyone can remember. You'll know it by its bright white bricks. It's believed to have healing properties left as a gift from the saints. People stopped using it quite some time ago, over fifty years, because though the well hasn't gone completely dry, the water is a long way down and gets further every passing year. Get the water from this well and this well only."

"If it's almost dry then how am I supposed to get the water?" Maritza's head was spinning as Abuela's words flew through her mind.

"I don't have all of the answers, but you have to find a way. Next, push forward into the mountains. You will come to an apple tree."

"An apple tree? Apples only grow in South Chile." Maritza interrupted.

"And that is how you'll know it's what you're looking for so take an apple from that tree. Stop interrupting," said Abuela in a terse voice. "Afterwards, find your way to a lush valley beneath the mountainside. It will be filled with rosemary. Pick a sprig that has fully matured. You remember what rosemary bushes look like?"

"Yes, but..."

"Good. Then you need salt. Our ancestors used to leave offerings in the temples of ancient times. Find the temple of Roca on the Sierra Nacer. It will be marked with a jaguar, retrieve the salt."

"Abuela, I don't think I can do this. I'm not

strong. Maybe there's still time to reach Papá," Maritza pleaded.

Maritza was losing the little courage she had. Abuela wasn't making sense. *Everything is happening too fast*, Maritza thought as she rocked back and forth to calm herself.

"And last," Abuela continued, her voice still strained, "high up the mountain, where the Río Serrano is nothing more than a trickle blooms the *rosa de palacio*. Few have ever seen one. It's rumored to bloom only at midnight so pick it then. The petals are plump and a deep red. They say it is so soft and delicate that the petals wilt if touched, so be careful."

Maritza looked down at the quipu resting in her hand, running a finger over each of the five knots. She was still unsure. *What if I forget something? What if I fail?*

"Mari," Abuela's voice had softened, "I know that I am asking too much of you, but this is not a time when we can afford to have doubt. Faith is what will push us on."

Abuela went over to the window and lit a candle. The sunlight highlighted the deep lines set into her face and the white of her thinning hair. She beckoned Maritza over and they both knelt and pressed their palms together. As Abuela prayed for Maritza's safe journey, Maritza struggled to shake the fear swelling inside of her. *How am I, at eleven years old, supposed to be trusted with the burden of saving Isidora, a girl turning to gold with every passing moment? Go on a journey? Alone?* It was too much, but what else could she do? Papá didn't even know what was happening to his girls. Maritza squeezed her palms tight as she asked for even an ounce more of strength. *Be strong Zita*, she wished.

"Amen," said Abuela.

"Amen," echoed Maritza as she rose.

"Remind me, what you need?" said Abuela.

"Water from the Mijas well, an apple from a tree, rosemary in a field, salt taken from a temple, and the *rosa de palacio* when it blooms at midnight," Maritza recited.

"Good girl, and you must be back before the new moon," warned Abuela, "it's time to go."

Abuela was always talking about horoscopes and moon cycles, so Maritza knew she didn't have more than a few days until the new moon. Maritza picked up Conejito from the table and snuggled him in the crook of Isidora's arm. Her little sister looked so peaceful in her sleep. A hint of a smile was spread on her lips. Like she had no idea of what was happening around her.

"Have only happy dreams," Maritza said, "and when I get back I'll tell you the greatest story of all."

She brushed Isidora's cheek and furrowed her brow as she took one last look at the golden fingers. She pulled on her red windbreaker and a yellow and red tassel hat before meeting Abuela at the door.

Abuela held up her *chanchito*. Maritza always thought the little clay pig was so funny looking with its three legs. But it was one of Abuela's superstitions that Maritza knew her to take very seriously. Abuela often had the family kiss the pig with the sunken eyes if she thought the weather looked poor, or if she'd had a bad dream. However, today Maritza knew she'd need all the luck she could get and she kissed the pig's cheek without any hesitation.

She stared up at Abuela's glossy gray eyes as she was fitted with her sack of meager supplies. They embraced and Maritza inhaled the sweet scent of Abuela's peony perfume as she pressed into her bosom. Abuela tied the rainbow quipu around Maritza's neck and hugged her once more.

"One more thing," Abuela said. "I don't know if this is true, but be careful of La Mujer Mojada. Ruana told me about her a few days ago. She said the woman comes cloaked in all black when the crickets sing. She leaves a trail of water in her path. But worse, there are murmurs that she snatches children who've strayed too far from their parents. I'm sure it's not true. We haven't had any missing children."

"How would I know if she were around?"

"They say crickets chirp when she is near, so listen carefully."

The only missing child right now was Isidora. Maritza longed for her little sister's smiling face. She needed more than anything to know that this was all an impossible dream. There were no Alicantos, no magic well water, no mysterious woman who snatches children. There was only her happy family, safe in Santa Alma telling stories just for fun.

Maritza looked once more to Isidora.

"Go now," Abuela said with one more kiss.

Maritza tucked the quipu beneath her shirt, along with the necklace holding Mamá's ring and she walked out into the night.

Chapter Six

As Maritza headed back up the steep path, leaving behind her home and her slumbering sister, she replayed the events of the day, wondering why any of this had happened. *Papá said the stories were true but he'd only been teasing*. Papá had wanted her to open up and make new friends. Instead she let Isidora nearly fall prey to a beast. *What kind of big sister am I? I should've protected her.*

When she came to the fork in the path she looked up to her left, towards the Alicanto's lair. She wondered if all the rumors about the cougar were really a lie to keep the children safe. *Surely Papá didn't think the Alicanto was real. He was kidding about the stories being real, but maybe the village Elders knew better?*

She remembered how the bird shrieked and stomped, flapping its molting wings in an attempt to escape. In that moment, and even now with the path before her, Maritza felt that same fear. She was beyond frightened of the chance that she couldn't save Isidora from the cave, and the fear hadn't left with her new task at hand. She and Isidora were still trapped. Thinking of the bird still trying to break free made her shudder.

Maritza picked up her pace and pushed down the path to Mijas. She'd never been there before, but she'd heard the village was sparkling and bustling with fat, happy people. Though she didn't have time for sightseeing, it might be a relief to see a cheerful face.

Not long after, the path opened up into a road and soon she stood in front of an alabaster sign.

"Welcome to Mijas
Be Kind and Merry"

 The words were engraved into the stone and were flanked on either side by bellflowers sticking up like trumpets.
 When Maritza passed the village threshold, she wasn't sure if she was disappointed or refreshed. What outsiders said of Mijas wasn't far from the truth. The homes and sparse buildings were indeed whitewashed and did seem even brighter when the sun hit them just right. The people were smiling and walking with a sense of purpose, but they were only chubby at best. Other than that, it didn't seem much different from Santa Alma. Maritza missed home already. She spotted the path across the courtyard leaving the village. She was only met with a few curious looks as she exited the square, passing another greeting sign that matched the first.

* * *

 Maritza traveled down the dusty dirt path,

humming to herself to pass the time. *A well with white stones,* she thought, *but everything seems so dry out here*. And indeed it was unusually dry considering she could see the Río Serrano was not even a mile away. The grass was almost all brown with small scattered patches of pale green. The only trees had thin, bare branches. Light dust was building up over her sneakers. She looked up at the sun which was beginning to sink and having seen no sign of the well, wondered if she should go back to spend the night in Mijas. Perhaps ask for directions. She was so distracted by this thought that she stumbled over something hard and landed smack on her knees, just barely sticking her arms out in time to keep from landing face first.

    She gritted her teeth as the pain stung the palms of her hands. She turned over sitting down to see what had caused her to take the tumble. She picked up the dust-caked object and wiped it off. Under the layer of dirt shone a pearly white brick. Maritza shot up squeezing the brick tight, and with her pain forgotten, she ran around the field searching for the well or even just another clue.

She spun and spun until she spotted it. In the distance surrounded by matted green grass she saw a hint of white and sprinted towards it, her sack bouncing on her back. When she reached it, she saw that it wasn't much of a well anymore. There was no rope or bucket, and over time the pristine brick walls had crumbled. White shards lay all around. Only one part of the wall was left intact and weeds crept between its cracks.

Maritza looked over the wall and down into the hole. It was pitch black and no water could be seen from where she stood. Staring down into the never ending darkness was disorienting. The excitement Maritza felt at finding the well had already begun to fade. *Now what?* she thought, *I've found the well but I'm no closer to getting the water for Isidora.*

She plopped down onto the grass and picked up one of the broken pieces of stone and tossed it up and down in her hand, she had an idea. *I can at least find out how deep it is and go from there.* Maritza stood and threw the shard into the abyss. She bent over the edge and listened carefully for a splash.

"Oww!" a voice rang up against the cool walls.

She scrambled back away from the well in shock. Was she in the sun too long? Was she going crazy?

"Hello? Is anybody out there?" the voice came again.

She was absolutely stunned and couldn't move or respond. A passing cloud cast a shadow over her and broke her from her stupor. *Someone's trapped!* she realized.

Maritza crawled her way back to the opening and peered down in hopes that the last rays of the day would let her see what was down there.

"Hello?" her voice barely came out above a whisper.

"I can see a shadow," the voice sounded youthful, but so tired. "Can you hear me?"

Maritza shook her head, realizing they must not have heard her. She needed to speak up. She balled her fist and tried again.

"I'm here!" she yelled into the black. "Are...are you hurt?"

"What is your name?"

"Uh..." Maritza was hesitant, "who are you?" her voice quivered.

"I am Fausto. I am not hurt, but can you please help me?"

"How did you get down there?"

"I fell, I am not sure when. It is too far for me to climb out."

There was a wet, slick, slapping against a hard surface, followed by a small splash. *He must have just tried to scale the wall,* Maritza thought. The sound reminded her of Papá's scary story and suddenly she felt the urge to run. But she couldn't do that, Isidora needed the water.

"Please," begged Fausto, "my family does not know where I am."

Maritza pressed her forehead to the brick. It was getting darker. This was impossible. *Could this be the boy from Papá's tale? How could anyone fall such a ways and survive? And if this is the boy from Papá's story, then he's been there for who knows how long*, she thought.

"Are you a ghost?" she asked.

"I..." he was hesitant, as though he never considered the possibility. "If I were I would have flown out of here long ago. And I get hurt if I fall too roughly. I am alive!"

I can't leave him here, she thought. *Even if he were a spirit, I still need the water.*

"There isn't anything to pull you up with," she said. "I have to go to town."

"No!" yelled Fausto. He sounded weak. "I do not remember the last time someone came by. Do not leave."

Unable to imagine what Fausto had experienced or for how long, Maritza was unsure of what to say. He needed freedom, and she needed the water. They needed to trust each other. *Isi would know what to say*, she thought. And that is what she tried.

"Trust me. I'm Maritza and I'm your friend now," she said doing her best to mimic Isidora's lighthearted kindness.

For a time there was silence and Maritza thought she'd ruined her chances already. Furthermore she didn't actually have a plan so what did she expect Fausto to say? Finally after what seemed like longer than either of them could spare, he called back.

"Okay," he said, with a hint of fear echoing off the walls.

"I'll be back soon," she promised. "I'll leave this here so you'll know I'm coming."

Maritza pulled out the candle from her sack. The glass was tall and slender with amber wax filled nearly to the top. She placed it on the top of the remaining white bricks and lit the wick.

* * *

Maritza ran back towards Mijas, feeling the weight of a second rescue mission. She eyed the sun. It burned a deep orange, only a few minutes of day left. Normally this sight was comforting to Maritza, it was the most beautiful. It reminded her of being out on the vineyard, but this time it only reminded her that she was one day closer to the new moon. One day closer to losing her Isidora.

Finally Mijas was in sight. But, what would she do when she got there? Start pounding on strangers' doors? How would she explain there was a boy stuck in a magical well that'd been there for however long? She'd slowed down to a trot going over everything in her head when she noticed a corral housing donkeys. On the gate post laid a tightly wrapped rope. It looked like it might be long enough. *I'll have to try it, but what can I attach it to?*

A donkey brayed in the corral and stomped its hoof in the muddy ground. *I guess there's no other way,* she thought as she recalled the emptiness of the well's field.

Maritza opened the corral and grabbed a leather harness. She approached the gray haired donkey, softly clicking her teeth. She reached out and petted the course hair down its neck. When she was sure it wouldn't shake her away she lifted the harness to its mouth for it to bite down. Maritza knew that whoever owned the homestead would be furious if they found her taking their livestock without permission, but she hoped they would understand she had lives to save.

She led the donkey out of the corral and slung the rope over her shoulder. It was thick and heavy, weighing her down, but she didn't have time to strap on a saddle. Fausto was alone and waiting in the dark.

* * *

The donkey followed her without much trouble, only sometimes trying to pull away. When she reached the well the candle was still glowing brightly.

"Fausto!" she called into the darkness.

"You came back!" his voice was more jovial than before.

"I got a donkey, and a rope. I'm going to pull you up, but I need you to do something," Maritza had not forgotten her original task. "That water down there, it's kept you alive right?"

"I think so. When I fell I broke my leg and hit my head, but after a few days in the water, both healed."

Maritza curled her toes in her shoes to hide her excitement. She opened her sack and dumped the water from the canteen Abuela had given her. She took off her coat, unwound the rope and made a running bowline knot just the way Papá had taught her. She opened the knot and slipped it around the donkey's neck. Hopefully the rope would be long enough. It was much longer than most ropes she'd used before at the vineyard, but the well was deep.

"Fausto," she called when she was ready, "I'm going to drop a canteen. Please fill it with the water. I need it for my sister, she's sick."

"Drop it down," he replied.

Maritza tossed the canteen into the well and felt a rush a relief when she heard it splash on the surface. Satisfied Fausto would keep his word as she'd kept hers, she blew out the candle and fed the rope down the shaft.

"Did you fill it?" she asked.

"Yes, and I feel the rope," he said. "It is a bit high but I can catch it if I jump. I am going to climb up."

The sandy rope disappeared as the tunnel grew darker but Maritza only felt glad that something in this troubled day was finally going right. The rope suddenly pulled tight under Fausto's weight which startled the donkey. It let out a strained bray and regained control of its footing. Maritza listened at the well for any sign of Fausto's footsteps, but heard nothing.

The donkey continued to bray and struggle under the unseen force every couple of moments, shaking its head and rearing. Maritza began to worry the animal was more skittish than she'd thought.

"Are you close?" she called.

No answer.

"Fausto?" she called again.

Maritza's chest tightened as the tension built up inside of her. The donkey was getting more and more spooked, and Fausto wasn't answering. *Maybe he hit his head again,* she panicked.

At that moment the donkey reared its head and shook itself free from the rope. The rope snaked rapidly towards the well as Fausto let out a howl. Maritza pounced on the rope and was only saved from falling in herself thanks to the short wall of remaining bricks. She clutched the rope tightly, bearing all of the weight, and craned her neck around to see the donkey running towards its home. At least she wouldn't have to explain taking the animal if it were already back.

    She pressed her shoulder to the wall and carefully slipped the knot around her waist. When she stood up the pressure from being pressed against the wall knocked the wind out of her, but she kept going. She held the rope tight, pulling it up the well wall with all of her strength, every inch a small victory. She gasped for air and pulled again. Her arms burned with the effort. Fausto was too quiet. She hoped she wasn't too late.

    Fearing the worst had happened to Fausto, Maritza gave the rope a hard tug and lost her footing, tipping over the edge of the wall that saved her life moments ago. As her toes lifted from the ground she snapped her eyes closed knowing she'd soon be plummeting down into the abyss. Thoughts of failure, Papá's disappointed face, and Isidora's golden body sped through her mind when a cold, wet, soggy hand latched onto her arm pushing her back.

    Maritza's feet were back in the dry grass. She opened her eyes to see a pair of sparkling blue eyes with gray flecks staring right back at her.

Chapter Seven

Maritza was frozen as Fausto's eyes bore into her. They seemed impossibly bright in the slim moon's light. He climbed the rest of the way out of the well and pulled her into a hug. He was soaking wet and smelled of sweat and damp moss. Maritza had never been this close to a boy before and almost too quickly pushed herself out of his grasp.

When she got a good look at him, Maritza

saw that Fausto didn't appear to be much older or taller than her, not even by a head. His limbs were slender, skinny even. He wore a gray shirt with frayed edges and a pair of ill-fitting beige pants. His skin was tanned like hers but he was a few shades lighter, he didn't get much sun after all. She trailed the waves in his longish, choppy hair. It looked like he'd been cutting the dark locks with a jagged stone. His eyes were wide and a bit sunken into his face, but he was smiling bigger than anyone Maritza had ever known, despite his ragged appearance.

"Thank you mi amor!" Fausto said as he stepped closer. "You are the most beautiful sight I have ever seen!"

He must've been down there a while, Maritza thought. *He sounds like one of Abuela's novellas.* His voice had a little dramatic flair and he spoke excitedly. She gazed at his thin arms again and figured he must have been hungry. In the moonlight his visage was haunting, but he was no ghost. She broke off a piece of bread and handed it to him. Fausto looked down at her outstretched hand

and his shoulders began to shake. Fearing she'd offended him Maritza pulled the bread back.

"I'm so sorry," she said.

"No, I am sorry," Fausto said in a cracked voice. "I have not had or seen food in so long, only that strange water day in and day out. I feared I would never eat again. And here you are, not only have you saved me, but you offer me this sweet bread. I cannot tell you how thankful I am. How could I possibly repay you?"

"You can have as much as you want. There's no need to...the canteen!" Maritza said, she'd nearly forgotten.

"Oh, this?" he replied. He handed the filled container to her and took the bread in return, stuffing his mouth. "This is nothing. You said you need it for your sister? Let me accompany you back home at least. Where do you live? You have to meet my parents, we don't have much but they will reward you."

This water has kept him young all these years. This is everything, she thought as she turned the canteen over in her hands. *It will save Isi.*

Maritza didn't know what to say. Fausto spoke with such ease to a complete stranger. He'd been alone for such a long time. The words burst out of him, desperate to reach ears that weren't his own.

"You said your sister is sick right?" he continued. "Then let us go. How far is it? I am from Mijas, are you?"

"No, I can't go home yet," she finally said. "I need the water for my sister, but I need a few other things as well. This was my first stop. Thank you for this, I have to get going."

"Hmm..." Fausto put his hand to his chin, "well I cannot send a young lady out on her own. I cannot ever thank you enough for saving me, but the least I can do is help you on your journey."

"It's okay, I'm sure your family misses you." Maritza said, trying to disguise the fact that she didn't want him to come. They'd just gone through an ordeal together, but still, he was a stranger. Right?

"They have waited this long they can wait a little longer. I must repay this debt. I insist, where are we going?"

Maritza tugged at the quipu around her neck thinking of his offer. *His family, if they're still alive would want him back. But, I don't want to continue alone. We're friends right? Friends should help each other.*

As she thought, Fausto started down the path away from Mijas and Maritza gathered her things to follow him.

"Maybe you should lead," he called back. "Where are we going?"

"I'm sorry, but no" she ran ahead. "I'm following the Río Serrano to the top. You are going home to find your family."

"Why?"

"Because, don't you miss them?" She couldn't let him come. She would have to talk to him. They'd be alone together. She didn't want him to see how ashamed and afraid she was. None of it was his concern.

"That is not what I meant, why are *we* following the Río Serrano?"

"I have to get things for my sister. Water, salt, things like that," she wasn't ready to reveal everything.

"Maritza, I am going to help you, I have decided. But I need to know how. If you have to go all the way to the beginning of the river, then your sister cannot have a normal illness. I have a sister too. I know you want to protect her. I would do the same, but everybody needs help."

"Then you should go see her," Maritza said, walking with her head down. *Why is he pushing me? I thought I told him to go home.*

"You said you were my friend back there," he said grabbing her shoulder. "I trusted you, you can trust me too. Let me be your friend."

Maritza turned with a sigh. She wasn't good at making friends. She didn't have Isidora's openness, or Paula's confidence. But Papá wanted her to try, and maybe she couldn't complete this task without help. She continued on the path only noting the sound of their footsteps.

"I'm warning you," she said facing Fausto, "this is going to sound crazy."

"I'm used to strange things," he said as he drew out his arms.

She took off the quipu and held it out,

telling Fausto how the Alicanto cursed Isidora, and how Abuela sent her out to find the cure. She couldn't bring herself to tell the thin boy how terribly she felt for letting Papá down and failing to keep Isidora safe. Some things she had to keep to herself.

Mamá had felt the same way once. Maybe even for a long time, but she gave Papá a chance and he was being an annoyance. Fausto only seemed to want to help.

Maritza knew her story sounded like a dark fairy tale. It sounded crazy. Nonetheless once she started, she couldn't stop until the whole story was out. She'd balled her fists so tightly that she could barely feel her fingertips.

Eyes forward, Maritza walked faster and faster. Fausto never interrupted her, not even for the odd question. He kept pace staying by her side.

When her story was complete, Maritza felt a weight lift off of her shoulders and she breathed easy, wiping away the few tears that'd fallen from her eyes. When she looked at Fausto again she expected to see judgment in his face. Instead she saw compassion, and fire.

His smile had not been removed. He looked like the same boy but he also now looked like someone who understood her, and Maritza was grateful to have shared her troubles. She felt a small smile spread across her own lips as the yellow knot fell loose from the quipu.

Chapter Eight

Maritza and Fausto walked through the night, chatting and learning about each other. Maritza mostly listened to Fausto's rambles. She found they didn't have many small things in common. She liked red while he liked blue, she was quiet and he was boisterous. But they both shared a love for the mountains they called home. They shared the joy of running through the foothills, eating shaved ice, reading Superman comics and gathering around the fire with friends and family.

What Maritza really enjoyed about Fausto's company was his impossible stories. They reminded her of Papá, though who was to say what was impossible after the day she'd had?

"One time, my church took a trip over the mountains and into Argentina," Fausto said. "When we were there the Padre bet a farmer that I could beat any of his steeds in a race! Can you believe it?"

"No, I can't," Maritza said with a smirk.

"Well, anyway," he continued, "the next morning, the farmer had gathered his best six horses. They were so tall and all muscle, but I wasn't scared."

"Of course you weren't."

"They lined us up in an open field. The smell, I promise, was worse than my *tía* Elena's liver soup. Bleh."

Maritza rolled her eyes as she stifled her laughter.

"The Padre held his gun up to the sky and shot it! I was off! I pushed my arms and legs so fast most of the horses did not stand a chance. The only one who could keep up with me was the all black Criollo named Lightning.

We were neck and neck and the finish line was in sight. I could feel the blisters growing on my feet. We kept pounding and crossed the line in a cloud of dust! When the dust settled everyone was cheering and saying for sure that I was the winner. There was a huge celebration that night!"

"If you finished in a cloud of dust how could they have seen who won?" Maritza teased.

"I am a strong man," Fausto said, skinny flexing his biceps. "Who else would have won?"

Maritza stared back at him before releasing the bubble of laughter she'd been holding back.

They'd made their way closer to the Río Serrano to stay on track. The moon was crossing the night sky with stars twinkling around it like diamonds. The sky was never that clear in the city.

Maritza knew that before too long it would be morning. She pointed out a large tree, and they stopped beneath it to get some sleep. She unfolded Papá's *chamanto*, and held it out for

Fausto to use as a blanket. But, like the gentleman he was, he refused the gesture and insisted she use it instead. He put on her tassel hat and jacket. The arms were too short on him, and the tassels looked like earrings, but he seemed happy enough. The two settled in, and listened to the buzzing song of the cicadas mixing with the deep croaks of the toads.

"Maritza, you said your Papá told you a story about me?" he said beneath the rustling leaves.

"He did," she answered. "He said his father told it to him. They call you *El Chico Pozo*. The story goes that you were born in the well. I didn't think you were real."

"I fell one day when I was playing. I wasn't paying attention."

"Papá has been telling that story since he was a boy himself."

"So it has been a long time," he was somber. "At least forty years. My family is likely gone. My mother and father..."

"You never know. We'll check when we get back," she said less confidently than she'd intended.

Maritza had never comforted anyone before. Even when Mamá passed, she wasn't old enough to sooth Papá. Today was the closest she'd ever come to consoling a grieving person.

"You are right," he said with a yawn. "I will not yet abandon hope. After all, you found me."

Maritza listened for his breathing to slow. He was only one year older than her. One year older when he fell into the well anyway, but he was resilient. She couldn't imagine what she would do if she'd been thrust into the world after so many years with only a prayer that she'd have a home to go back to. Isidora, Abuela, and Papá were her world. Without them, who would she be?

Fausto was finally quiet. All that could be heard was the wind, and the chirping of crickets in the distance. *It's nothing to be worried about*, Maritza thought as she caressed Mamá's ring. *We're always together*. When she was sure he'd fallen asleep, she let the night claim her as well.

* * *

Maritza opened her groggy eyes as warm sunbeams darted through the branches. It took her a moment to realize where she was. She'd dreamt of Isidora, but it was the kind of dream that was more of a memory. Papá had taken the girls to town and let them play video games at an arcade. Isidora wanted to play with the pinball machine, but she was too small to see all the blinking lights.

Maritza came to the rescue with an overturned a milk crate for Isidora to stand on. They put coin after coin into the machine. Isidora loved to pull the spring to get the game started. Maritza liked to pull it too, but she let Isidora do it every time just to see her glowing smile. The girls laughed along to the music and frantically triggered the flickers to keep the ball in play. Maritza had taken the tickets they'd won from the machine and traded them in for Conejito. All Maritza wanted to do was go back home back to that day. She never thought she'd ever have to worry about losing her sister.

Maritza sat upright and stretched out her

arms. She could see Fausto down at the river bed shaking out his wet hair. The moist beads caught the shine of the sun. As he grinned over his shoulder at her, she quickly looked away.

I have the water, she thought, shaking off the unexplained embarrassment she felt. *Next I need to find the apple tree.* She needed to get a clear view of her surroundings and raised her sights to the tree she'd slept under. At home, she and Isidora loved to climb the trees around the village, but she'd never climbed one this high.

The tree more than towered over her frame. The branches were thick and twisted, abundant with lush green leaves. She stepped onto a protruding root that she'd used as a pillow and took grab of a knot. She tried to gain leverage reaching for the lowest branch, but she was too short.

"Whoa, whoa!" cried Fausto from behind her. "What are you doing?"

"I'm climbing the tree to see where we are," she said continuing to reach without success.

"It is dangerous, get down. I will go."

"No thank you, I've got it."

Maritza heard Fausto suck his teeth, before he grabbed her legs and gave her a lift upward.

"Hey!" she protested.

"Do not squirm. Hurry and grab the branch."

She did so and swung herself up. After calling back a thanks she climbed higher into the tree, testing each branch with a tap of her foot. The tree was sturdy and her light weight helped her reach the thinner limbs. Before long, she poked her head out of the top and took in the vast landscape.

Behind her were the daunting mountains capped with powdery snow. Below were green fields with scattered wildflowers of every color. Birds flew overhead, occasionally diving into the river to snag a fish for breakfast. Maritza's stomach rumbled at the thought. Further upward, she saw a tightly bound cluster of trees at the foothills that appeared to be aligned in a perfect circle.

They were too far to tell what kind of trees they were, but Maritza decided they would be her next stop. She climbed back down and when she made it to the bottom branch, Fausto held out his frail arms to catch her. Maritza gave him a stern look. He simply smiled and raised his eyebrow. Maritza couldn't help but chuckle at his gesture and swung down so she was closer to the ground before she jumped to him.

Even though she'd moved lower, her weight knocked him down and they both rolled around in the grass laughing.

"I suppose I am not yet back to my normal strength," he said taking deep breaths. "You know, when my friends and I played stick ball, I could whack the ball clear across the cornfield!"

"Sure," she retorted. "And Peter Pan once crept through my window and taught me how to fly!"

They burst into another fit of laughter. It felt good for Maritza to laugh. She wanted it to last longer, but they had to move on. They ate more of the bread and grapes before heading towards the trees.

* * *

The circle of trees was much larger and denser than Maritza originally suspected. She and Fausto had to squeeze through the tightly grown trees. There was no defining path and they found themselves passing by the same trees over and over as though they were in a maze. Every time they came to the tree with mushrooms around it, Maritza kicked at the trunk. They wove in and out, snagging their clothes on twigs, for what seemed like forever. Maritza could not tell though because the thick leaves blocked out the sun.

Finally, they pushed into a clearing at the center of the ring. Fausto's face was beet red. Maritza realized he'd been in the dark so long, the trees probably made him feel as though he were confined in the well again.

Soon however, he was smiling again and pointed behind her. Maritza turned around to find a single tree up a small incline of the curled grass. Scattered around the base were the remnants of fallen pink blossoms. The tree had rough bark that was a mixture of grays and browns and the trunk was curved like an hourglass. It stood straight up and the branches pointed upwards to the clear sky. Maritza stepped back to catch sight of the top, and there she saw them. Shining red apples graced the upper branches of the tree. Fausto must've known what the smile across her face meant.

"Another boost Madam?" he said.

Maritza gladly accepted his offer and eagerly stepped into his cupped hands. As soon as she began to climb, the tree bent over and a branch swept towards her and knocked her back to the ground. *What on earth?* she thought. Her rear stung from the fall. The tree straightened itself and just below the crown the bark was quivering. Slowly a large oval pushed out of the bark. A bump formed in the middle of the oval, which reminded Maritza of a nose. A small mouth with full lips followed, and finally a pair of closed curved eyes. The bark did nothing to mar the beauty of the countenance. While Maritza was lost in elegant face that had taken shape, the eyes flickered open.

"Well I have never," the tree spoke. "Little girl climbing on face! How rude!"

Maritza and Fausto jumped away from the talking tree. They looked around expecting the other trees to spring to life as well. But nothing happened. Turning their eyes back to the apple tree, Fausto pushed Maritza forward and she snapped her head back giving him a deep glare.

"You need the apple," he said shrugging his shoulders.

"Come here little girl," said the tree. "Let me look at you."

"What...who are you?" Maritza asked as she moved forward, hesitating with each step.

"Who am I?" asked the tree. "You are climbing on *my* face. I think I should be the one asking who you are."

"I'm so sorry," gasped Maritza. "I didn't know Miss...who are you again?"

"Well that is quite the tale. Would you like to hear it?"

Maritza felt there was no time for a story. There were only a few days left until the new moon. She really wanted to beg for the apple and move on. *She already thinks I'm rude,* she thought. *Maybe if I tell her about Isidora she'll give me an apple.*

Fausto placed a hand on her should interrupting her thoughts. The gentle smile on his lips quelled her growing anxiety. She turned back to the tree and nodded her head as she and Fausto sat on the ground and waited. The tree's lips stretched into a smirk, enhancing her beauty, and she began:

"I came from a faraway land across a vast blue ocean. I was fourth of seven sisters, and our father was the Peha. *I believe you use the word 'king.' Making me a* Gong Joo, *or as you would say 'princess.'*

Growing up I had anything a young girl wanted. A grand red palace with pavilions and gardens, elegant silk dresses, jewels adorning my hair, more servants and playthings than I knew what to do with. Even my tutor had to do whatever I told him. When I didn't want to practice calligraphy, I made him draw. When I grew bored with arithmetic, I ordered him to sing instead. I continued like this well into my adolescence. It was a good life, but sometimes the nobles chastised me. And they had Peha's *favor.*

'Gong Joo, Gong Joo,' they would say. 'You must be educated. You must fulfill your honorable duties.'

'You are right nobles,' I would say every time, lowering my eyes. 'Tomorrow I will be new.'

And each new day I would be up to the same tricks. Finally, one day I was walking through the palace halls with my ladies in waiting. I'd decided to forgo my poetry lesson. When I came to pass Peha's *chambers, I heard voices within. Although I was already being naughty I decided to press my ear to the paper wall and listen in.*

*'*Peha, Gong Joo *has not improved,' said the noble. 'How will we be able to present her at the betrothing ceremony?'*

'I am torn,' said my father. 'She is a wild spirit and I want all of my daughters to be happy. But she, like her sisters before her, must fulfill her duty to Korea. In the next year, she will be married.'

Hearing this I picked up my skirts and ran towards my chambers. I heard the door to father's room slide open, but I couldn't look back. When I got to my room I dismissed the maids and bolted the door. In my bed I cried and cried until I'd run out of tears. I knew that my older sisters had been forced into marriage to keep our country unified, but they were not in love and I would not do the same.

There was a medicine woman in the palace. She supplied all remedies when we were tired or sick. She used to adore me when I was a child and would try to teach me about herbs. I was not very kind to her however. I would sometimes replace her makeup jars with chalk and I once even put a mouse in her bed pillow. Since then there was a grimace behind the smile on her face whenever she saw me. But, she could never speak out against a princess.

I figured she could help me. Give me a potion to change Peha's *mind. Anything so that I could make my own choices. When I entered her room she was peddling through the stores of herbs. She was a larger woman in a green cloth robe. When she saw me alone, she let her disdain for me show. I sat and told her that I needed something so that I wouldn't have to get married. At this a smile came across her face. I had not expected that she would want to help me. But what could she do? She knew she was bound to accept a royal order.*

She put mixed herbs into a stone bowl and ground them into a dust. She then threw the powder into a small cauldron over a fire. A puff of purple smoke came up from the pot and when it cleared, the medicine woman reached in and pulled out a dark red apple.

'Eat this, and you will never marry,' she said as she handed the fruit to me.

I hid it in my sleeve and thanked her before leaving. In the hall I was met by one of the nobles.

'Gong Joo, Peha says you deserve a trip. You will tour South America to learn about their agriculture and Jae-Hwa will escort you. You will leave in three days.'

We took a ship here to your country. We were on the voyage for months. Jae-Hwa kept trying to make conversation with me, but I was not interested. He was the son of a noble. I remembered him wanting to play with me when we were children, but I never did because his face and clothes were always dirty from playing too roughly outside.

One night we were having the evening meal in a small town and he confessed to me.

'Gong Joo,' he said. 'There is something I want to tell you. It is happy news. Peha has chosen me as your betrothed. I will be most honored to have you as my bride.'

When he was finished he stood and bowed to me. I was stunned. We were not here to learn about farming, he was wooing me! Peha had betrayed me, and I had told him I didn't like Jae-Hwa! And even more, my own father couldn't tell me himself.

I felt the hidden apple I always kept on my person and ran out of the mud brick house. Jae-Hwa ran after me but at the edge of the town I lost him by jumping into a row of trees. I kept running through the night and into the next day. I followed the mountains and the river, not going anywhere in particular until I found this circle of trees. I pushed my way through and sat on this little hill, completely embarrassed by my behavior but not ready to go back either. Peha *had forced my hand. I raised the apple knowing now that it was the only way to change his mind.*

I ate the entire apple, even the core, desperate for it to work its magic and fell asleep beneath the warm sun. It was the worst mistake of my life for when I awoke my arms were stiff and sticking straight out. I stood in a daze and my feet sank into the ground where I could not move them. My body stretched up towards the sky and my skin became dark and hard. The medicine woman had tricked me! She said I would never marry and she was right, because one hundred years ago, she turned me into this tree."

Maritza and Fausto stared with wide eyes. *This is the true version of Isi's favorite story,* Maritza thought. *It's not like how Papá said. He told us the princess ate too many mud pies. That the princess was a little girl who lived happily ever after. All his stories end happily. Will mine? I hope I get to tell Isi.*

Feeling satisfied she'd been polite by listening to the princess's tale, she approached her again. There wasn't much time and Isidora was waiting.

"*Gong Joo*," she said with a curtsey, "I'm sorry for being rude earlier. It's just that I'm in a hurry. My sister Isidora has been cursed too and I need one of your apples to save her. I was supposed to take care of her, but I was careless and now she's in danger! I can't let her down again."

"One of my apples?" asked the princess. A smirk curved on her lips and her eyebrows lifted as though she had a thought. "If you want one of my apples, you must do something else first. I was not wise as a child, but perhaps you are. Solve this riddle and tell me my name. Do this, and the apple is yours:

When the sun and moon no longer rise
and the Earth has crumbled to dust,
The Creator and time will be what's left
and I by their side."

Maritza went over the words in her head *no sun, no moon, no Earth. The Creator and time will be what's left. So no stars or planets either.* She turned to Fausto who just shook his head. *No ideas there,* she thought. The sun was high up in the sky now. *What happens when everything is gone? Sister Maria says when we die a special part of us lives on and it's eternal.* Ready to try her answer, Maritza looked into the princess's wooden eyes.

"Eternity," she said.

The princess's smile remained as she bent down putting the apples in Maritza's reach. Maritza plucked the fruit and put it into her sack as the princess straightened.

"In Korea the word for 'eternal' is 'Young'" said the princess. "That is what I am called."

"Thank you Princess Young," said Maritza.

"But, be warned. Do not use the core. I did learn from that wretched medicine woman that apple seeds contain poison, the seeds in my apple are not safe to eat."

"I won't."

"You are a clever girl," Young continued. "Your mother and father must be proud."

Maritza touched Mamá's necklace beneath the quipu at the kind words, and beneath her fingers, the blue knot unraveled.

"Maybe after I save my sister I can find a way to save you," she said to Young.

"No, I made my choice," said Young, "I should have been kinder and not acted so foolishly. This is my punishment. And here, surrounded by the beauty of nature, I am happier than I ever pretended to be before. But, it is lonely. If you would like to visit sometime and tell me of the world, I would be grateful."

"I will, and I'll bring my sister," Maritza said as she clutched onto the bag.

Proud, Papá had told Maritza that he was proud of her many times, but what would he think now? Maybe if it weren't for Maritza, Isidora would've never gotten ill. She would've never left the village. Everyone would be safe at home, maybe listening to the radio with Abuela.

And what about Mamá? Maritza would never know if Mamá was proud of her. She only got to spend moments with Isidora, so that means Maritza should have worked even harder every day to make sure she was safe and taken care of.

I have to make this right, she turned to leave.

"One more thing," said Princess Young, pulling Maritza from her thoughts.

"Yes princess?"

"What is your name little girl?"

"Maritza."

"Thank you Maritza," Young said as Maritza and Fausto disappeared through the trees.

Chapter Nine

Two down, three to go, Maritza thought as she and Fausto broke through the last line of trees. The peaked sun washed over her face and reflected off of the steady river. She shielded her eyes and looked into the distance at the looming mountain which she hoped was the true source of the Río Serrano. Abuela hadn't been incredibly specific. How could she be? It's amazing that she knew as much as she did to begin with.

No one travels this far. There isn't anything out here. For all I know, the river could go over the Sierra Nacer and into Argentina.

As they continued along the river Maritza kept an eye out for the rosemary field. The air was fresh and the sun gave pleasant warmth. The path was covered with vibrant green grass. Every once in a while, she would spot fish jumping upstream from the water. The shine of their scales and small splashes gave her small moments of happiness, but she couldn't be too distracted.

Hours passed and she worried that she'd already missed the field. Fausto hadn't spoken for a while either. He was normally telling some ridiculous story of how he wrestled a bear or lifted a truck off of a child's toy. She shook her head and grinned at the thought, but after what she'd seen the in past couple of days maybe anything was possible. She turned around to check on him and he ran up and knelt before her.

"For you my lady," he said. He was holding a band of white alstroemeria, or Lily of the Incas flowers. He raised and placed the band on her head. "A crown for the princess. All hail Princess Zita!"

Maritza's cheeks flushed red as a cherry and she clasped her hands over her mouth to trap the gasp that wanted to escape. Only Mamá had ever called her Zita. And just what was Fausto up to? Was he trying to embarrass her?

Before she could say a word Fausto sprinted past her, laughing all the way. Maritza's heart thumped against her chest as he passed by her, his scent floating on the wind, and she felt an emptiness when he was gone. She caressed the delicate petals in her hair.

She took a moment to gather herself, shaking off the unfamiliar tingling in her belly. She sucked in a breath and bit down on her lip. *He's just a boy. There's lots of boys back home.*

When she was ready to get moving again, she noticed Fausto had ran quite a distance ahead of her and was looking across the river and pointing. She jogged to catch up and was panting by the time she saw what he'd spotted.

Clear across the river was a small meadow enclosed by a passage of clustered rocks. In the meadow Maritza could see a sprinkling of what looked like violet sprouts. *Rosemary,* and as she had the thought, a brisk minty aroma carried on the wind and pummeled her senses.

"I hope that you are fair at swimming," said Fausto.

"Um, actually, I'm not," she responded, breaking free from the rosemary's spell.

Maritza looked up and down the river, no bridge.

"There's no way across," she said. "What are we going to do?"

"It is okay because look," he took her head in his warm hands and pointed her downstream. "There are some rocks sticking out that you can grab onto."

"Oh no, no, no!"

"Swimming is easy! Here, I will show you."

"Absolutely not. The water is moving much too fast. We'll never make it."

"Like you said, there is no other way across."

Fausto took off his shoes, leaving them on the bank. He rolled up his pant legs and stepped into the water. He wobbled a bit against the current, but it was evident that he was gaining his strength. He walked deeper into the river until his waist was covered and started swimming upstream, fiercely kicking his legs and paddling his arms. Against the current, he looked to be swimming in place. When finished with his demonstration, he stood back up and got out of the river like he'd done something as simple as opening a door. Maritza was not convinced. The water was a deep blue, and still looked too wide to cross safely.

"See it is easy! I will carry the satchel and help you," Fausto said. "All you are going to do is kick your feet very hard and grab onto the rocks. I will swim across and pull you out. Take off your clothes and put them in here."

Fausto removed his shirt and stuffed his things into the sack. When he held it out to Maritza she stood frozen at his lack of modesty. No way would she undress in front of a boy! She slipped off her shoes and jacket averting her view from his bare chest. She did as he had done and rolled up the legs of her jeans.

He linked his still cool hand through hers and led her into the water. It was beyond chilled and sent a shiver up her spine. The wind had picked up but the current wasn't as heavy as she expected. Mud squished between her toes as they walked deeper hand in hand.

"Now, lift your feet and kick quickly," Fausto said as he grabbed her other hand and faced her towards him.

She looked into his eyes, summoning the courage to trust him with her life. Isidora was counting on her, and now she was counting on him. The river was thinner than she guessed, certainly thinner than it was closer to Mijas and Santa Alma. The rosemary was not that far away. And Fausto knew what he was talking about, right? He'd spent years living in a well, in water. With that in mind, she let her feet be swept up and clutched Fausto tight. The river came in a rush and she held on tighter. Grainy water splashed up over her face and into her nose, causing her to cough.

"Kick! Kick!" she heard Fausto yelling.

Maritza kicked and kicked her feet trying to find a rhythm and when she did she found she stayed closer to the surface more easily. After she'd gotten more comfortable, Fausto pulled her back to the bank.

"See? Not so bad," he said as he sat down on the grass.

"I've never been swimming before. Thank you," she said. "How did you learn?"

"My father taught me," Fausto looked down between his legs hiding his face. "Alright, well let us go. We cannot waste the daylight!"

He jumped up and swung the bulging sack around his torso. His chipper demeanor had returned. Maritza had glimpsed the change in him, but decided to put it aside for the time being. He was right. They had to cover as much ground as possible.

They stepped back into the water and Fausto gestured downstream. There were three stones for Maritza to grab onto. The third was significantly smaller than the other two. She had no room for error. *Okay Zita, you can do this. Kick really hard, paddle, and grab the rocks. Fausto will be right there.*

"I am going to swim ahead," Fausto said, and before Maritza could protest, he dove in.

She couldn't let him get too far so she mustered up her strength and followed. The river took her swiftly. It felt much stronger than when Fausto was her anchor. *Kick!* She flailed her arms and feet, again finding a rhythm as she drifted at an angle. The first rock came up and Maritza latched on with a thud. Catching her breath, she hugged onto it. The course stone had been baking in the sun and Maritza's cheek was warm as cold water splashed against her back.

    She lifted her head to find Fausto. He was still upstream from her looking back. His legs and arms moved about desperately, but his face was calm. *Okay, only two more*, she thought briefly before plunging once again into the current. *Kick, kick, kick,* she told her herself over and over again. Her arms and legs were burning with muscles she never knew she had. She slammed into the second rock, just as hot as the other.

    Her hair stuck in thick locks to her face. Maritza pushed aside the thick ropes of hair and found white petals sticking to her fingers. Patting the top of her head, she found nothing there. Squinting her eyes she searched downstream. Maritza's heart sank and she slumped her shoulders as she watched the crown of flowers Fausto made for her float down into the distance.

Last one, she thought as she turned to the final stone. There were more important things to worry about right now, like making sure she didn't float away like her beautiful flowers.

The final rock was short, barely a few inches above the water. Fausto was already on the bank beckoning her forward. Maritza felt the hairs on the back of her neck prickle. What if she missed? How far would she be carried away? She could even drown. But she had to take the chance.

*One...two...three...*she leapt off and kicked as hard as she could towards the bank. *There it is!* She grabbed at the rock and clutched it with one hand, but it was slick and slipped through her fingers.

That's it, she thought fleetingly, *I'm sorry Isi.* But not more than a moment later she felt a hand wrap around her flailing wrist.

Between the waves of water washing over her face, Maritza saw Fausto grinning down at her.

"Are you not glad I came?" he said with a wicked tinge.

He reached for her other arm and pulled her out of the Río Serrano. Maritza could not stop herself. She pushed against Fausto hugging him close.

They'd made it.

Chapter Ten

Maritza jumped away from Fausto after regaining her senses. Fausto snickered as he patted her head and she was reminded that she'd lost his beautiful crown. She smoothed down her hair, suddenly concerned with how she looked.

They were both soaked to the bone but to Maritza, the drops of water clinging to Fausto were like fresh morning dew.

"Thank you Fausto," she said. "Yes, I'm glad you came."

"I believe that is twice I have saved your

life," he laughed.

"I'll pay you back somehow."

"Even if I saved you a thousand times, that could not compare to the years of solitude that you rescued me from."

"Well to be fair," Maritza said with a roll of her eyes, "it's not like I knew I was going to save you."

Fausto squinted at her and kicked up a splash of water from the river.

"Time to dry off Princess Zita!"

"Time to keep moving you mean," she said wiping the water from her face.

"We will catch cold, and we have been through a lot today. We should rest."

But Maritza was already walking towards the meadow. The rosemary was in sight and she wasn't going to slow down now. Fausto had no choice but to grab the sack and follow suit.

"Why can't we rest?" he called. "Your sister is sick, you cannot get sick as well."

"I have to be home by the new moon," she answered. "That's only two days away."

Only two days. Saying it out loud made the deadline seem all the much closer to Maritza and she burst into a full sprint. Her wet jeans were heavy and tight but she kept pumping her aching legs. When she reached the dark rocks of the meadow she leaned against one to catch her breath. Her palms were sweating and the clouds seemed to swirl above her. *Only two days left,* she thought, *and I only have two of the items. Isidora is probably half gold by now and I don't even know if Papá has come back home!* Maritza paced around in circles and pushed her hair back frantically, fretting over the looming new moon.

"See Zita, we are here. It took no time. You need to calm down," panted Fausto as he finally caught up. "Besides look at that tree up there. It hangs over the river, wouldn't it be fun to jump in from there now that you can swim, sort of?" he joked.

"Stop it Fausto!" Maritza screamed. Her words were steamed in rage "Don't you get it? Isidora is just a little girl and she's turning to gold. If I don't hurry she will die! We already lost Mamá, we can't lose Isi too. And you, you're just like her. You just laugh and have fun all the time and you don't think of the consequences!"

Maritza slumped down against the cold rock and wept into her hands. *It's too much Abuela. Why did you make me do this? Why didn't you let me find Papá?* She ripped up a tuft of grass and threw it towards the river. She'd never felt this mix of fear, anger, and sorrow before. Along with the pressing guilt she already felt, she didn't know what to do with the ugly things bursting out of her. Rapid waves of chirps invaded her, pounding against her eardrums like gravel. She could feel the cricket legs crawling up her arms.

"Shut up!" she screamed.

"I am sorry," Fausto said as he wrapped his arm around her shoulder. She pulled away. "It must be hard. I did not mean to be insensitive. I just want to help, and take care of you."

Maritza sat in silence, heaving on her sobs. She knew she should apologize, but she wasn't ready yet. The feelings were too raw.

"That tree ahead isn't very far away. We can rest there for tonight. I'll go ahead to dry out our things and build a fire so you can be alone."

When Fausto left Maritza's anger lingered, but not at Fausto or Abuela. She'd overreacted. Fausto only wanted to be her friend and stay by her side. In return she let her fear rule her. *But not anymore.* She vowed to herself that she would stop acting like a baby and instead be strong. And the first thing she wanted to do with her new found strength was admit to Fausto that she was wrong.

She got up and wiped her face, ready to follow Fausto, but she figured she may as well grab the rosemary while she was there. She peeked into the small meadow hoping to spot a good sprig. She'd seen lots of purple sprouts from across the river, but close up she realized that's exactly what they were, sprouts.

Abuela said I need a mature sprig, fully grown. Where are they? As Maritza looked deeper into the meadow she heard a rustling among the bushes. *Just the wind on the branches,* she thought but as she looked on, the bushes bent away from each other as though creating a path.

Bushes creaked and snapped back in the meadow in a long curling pattern. A smooth obsidian oval popped up from the rosemary. It rose higher and higher and Maritza realized it was connected to a slick limbless body. *A snake!* The snake was large and thick. Maritza had never seen such a colossal creature. Not even when her school had taken a trip to the zoo. With the snake's long tail, it seemed to be even larger than the monstrous Alicanto.

The beast's belly was a pale sickly cream, but its scales were magnificent. The small diamonds on its back cascaded like a rainbow fading from red to green to yellow. And even more they were coated in a pearly film that radiated all sorts of colors. The eyes were a fluorescent yellow with sleek black slits and they were topped with what looked like fleshy eyelashes.

Maritza let out a sigh as she marveled at the entrancing figure. Unsure of whether the snake would be a friend or foe, she tucked behind a rock to keep herself out of sight. The last time she met a beast such as this, Isidora was cursed. But, Maritza was not afraid and she held her ground. She was ready to wait the snake out and claim the territory. However, she decided to watch the snake to see what she was up against.

> *"I'm the beauty of the sea*
> *Not one is my rival*
> *I outshine even the sssun*
> *And it hides from me in shame*
>
> *Many have sailed to take my ssskin*
> *I've braved the storm and sunken ships*
> *I've slain the best and devoured them whole*
> *I'm the beauty of the ssssea."*

Though she was surprised, Maritza did not flinch through the dreadful lullaby. She hadn't expected the snake to speak, much less sing, but she vowed not to show weakness. She looked past the snake and saw three rosemary bushes filled with matured lavender blooms. Pushing aside the warning in the song, Maritza pulled back her shoulders and walked up to the snake.

"Excuse me, I need passage," Maritza said in the shadow of the snake.

"Why have you tresssspassed in Hasna's fieldsss?" asked the snake when it noticed the girl below.

"I don't know anyone called Hasna," Maritza answered the snake's hiss, "but, I simply need one of those rosemary sprigs there."

"You will have to look sssomeplace elsssssssse," said the snake as she batted her wispy lashes.

"My sister is s⁻..."

"Hasssssna does not care about your sssister!" the snake interrupted, rising even higher above Maritza. "Hasna is the most beautiful creature that has ever lived and I dessserve the most beautiful blossoms! They are mine! Mine! Mine!"

The snake bared her fangs and Maritza sucked in a breath as venom dripped from the stark spikes onto the ground beneath her. She clamped her fist and steadied her breathing. *I guess she must be Hasna,* she thought, *I can't defeat her in a fight. I'll have to try something else.* Maritza shifted her eyes careful not to move, looking for something she could use. She heard the tweets of birds flying above and the roar of the river behind her. The bushes tickled her legs with the blowing wind.

"Are you sure you can't spare just one?" Maritza asked in hopes her plan would work.

Hasna darted around Maritza in a flash. She wrapped herself in coils around the girl's tiny frame. Maritza balled her fists as the beautiful but deadly scales locked around her over and over squeezing her chest. She coughed out a gasp but kept her resolve. *No fear,* she told herself as the cold snake tightened its grip.

"How dare you! It's been quite some time since I've eaten a human. Maybe I should have a ssssweet child as my meal tonight?" hissed the snake. "You should have left when I gave you the chance!"

Hasna raised her head and unhinged her jaw with a sickening crack. Maritza looked into the deep red of Hasna mouth. Poison dripped from the dagger like teeth into Maritza's already matted hair. Hasna drew herself back to strike.

"Don't worry," said Hasna, "you are lucky. When I eat you, you will become a part of me."

"Wait!" Maritza forced out the word.

"Inssssolent child," Hasna said as she loosened her hold on Maritza. "You think you can invade my home, the home of the most beautiful and fearsome being, and take what you want?"

"How can you even be sure that you're the most beautiful?" Maritza asked sucking in what little air she could. "I mean, I heard you singing. You used to live in the sea. There aren't any mirrors there. Have you ever even seen yourself?"

"Shut your disgusting mouth you little sneak! While I have not seen my face, I have seen my shining tail every day. There could never be anything more lovely. It is beautiful so surely I am beautiful."

"You are lovely, but I've seen something more beautiful," Maritza said putting her plan in motion.

"More beautiful than me!" cried the snake.

"You're quite brave to say such things! Or perhaps, you are a fool."

"I have! Only a little while ago. I can show you," Maritza continued.

Hasna uncoiled herself from Maritza. The girl took a deep breath when she was finally free. Hasna slithered around Maritza sticking out her forked tongue. She rose above Maritza once more.

"If it is so, I will crush whatever being you speak of and I again will reign as the supreme beauty of land *and* sea."

"You won't be disappointed. It isn't far, follow me."

Maritza didn't want to turn her back on the obsessed creature, but she willed herself to pick up her feet and stepped out of the meadow towards the river. As she headed downstream, she heard the snake's belly sliding across the grass. *This is my only chance.* Maritza swallowed hard as she stopped at the riverbank.

"Well?" Hasna asked as she propped herself up. "I don't ssssee anything. If you have lied, you will be my meal inssstead." Venom dropped from her fangs, covering the ground in the viscous liquid.

"You have to look, there," said Maritza as she pointed to the flowing, but smooth surface of the water.

"Oh my," said the snake as she peered into the river.

Hasna stood tall with the sun radiating off her scales as she stood in a daze on the riverbed. The snake crept closer to the edge staring down. Maritza blew a light whistle, testing if the snake would notice her, but the serpent did not move. Hasna simply swayed her head side to side keeping her vision fixated on the image before her. Maritza bit her lower lip to compress the rush of excitement in her. She had guessed from Hasna's song and what she said about deserving the flowers, that the snake was so vain she would be enchanted by her own reflection, and Maritza was right. She backed her way to the meadow and grabbed the rosemary she sought. When she turned back the check if Hasna had spotted her theft, all she saw was a shimmering tail slipping into the current.

Chapter Eleven

Maritza finally made it to the tree Fausto had made camp beneath. It wasn't very tall, but the trunk was so thick her whole family could fit around it. The branches reached far out and were covered with small bushels of leaves. He had gotten much further than she'd thought. *He must've been pretty upset.* Their clothes and Papá's *chamanto* were lying in the grass in a line drying under the sun. Fausto was beneath the shade. He had managed to start a fire and was cooking something on a stick. *Just apologize, it's the right thing to do*, she told herself. She clutched the sprig of rosemary in her hand and made her way over.

"Your matches got wet," Fausto said when he noticed her just standing there. "And the bread did not make it."

He wasn't smiling, Maritza noticed as she sat beside him. Now that she was closer she saw he was twirling a fish over the fire. Her stomach rumbled. They had been eating sparingly. *He saved me from falling into the well, helped me into the tree, and saved me from the river, and now food and warmth. He really has taken care of me.*

"I'm sorry that I yelled," she began. When Fausto didn't say anything she continued. "I didn't mean what I said back there. I just got scared. I'm still ashamed that I let Isi get hurt. I don't know what's happening at home. Abuela sent me out here, but she doesn't know everything. I don't have much time left, and I'm still not sure any of this will work if I do get back. We can't lose her. Especially Papá. Mamá died when Isi was born. Besides one faded picture and this ring, Isi is all we have left of her."

Maritza removed the golden ring stamped with a rose from her neck and held it out for Fausto to see. He finally turned away from the fire. He reached out and touched the ring. Maritza felt a slight twinge. He was touching a part of her and she'd never felt so vulnerable. Fausto must have sensed this for he quickly moved on.

"It is okay," he said. "I see you got the rosemary. I am glad that you did not have any trouble."

"Actually!" Maritza breathed, happy to move on to a new subject. "There was a snake. You should have seen her! She was huge. Bigger than me and colorful and she had eyelashes!"

"What? What happened? Did it bite you?"

"Almost! I didn't run though. I tricked her, and when she was distracted I swiped up the rosemary and came here!"

"Wow..." his eyes were wide. "You crossed a

river not knowing how to swim and took on a giant snake by yourself? You have certainly been fearless today Zita."

As Fausto turned back to the roasting fish, Maritza felt a sense of pride. As she wrapped the chained ring back around her neck, she noticed a straight red string. The quipu had one less knot.

* * *

Maritza woke with a yawn as dawn arrived. She was glad she'd listened to reason. They'd spent the night under the tree. The fish Fausto made with the remaining grapes was the best meal they'd had. He even managed to catch a few more fish to take with them. Maritza was in better spirits and laughed at the memory of him jumping from an outstretched branch into the river. The small break was a relief, and she certainly didn't want to spend the night in the cold mountains, which was where they were going next.

She shook Fausto to wake him and he threw out his arm in protest. He'd been working hard too, but when Maritza dropped water on him from her cupped hands, he couldn't resist her. With their things dried and repacked, they started towards the mountain in the distance.

"So we are going to a mountain for salt?" Fausto said. After walking for a while he was fully awake. "Seems like a strange place for salt."

"It's all strange," Maritza said. "But it's actually a temple that we're going to. Abuela said it's marked with a jaguar. Have you ever heard of it?"

"No, I just hope it is not too high. At least we found the beginning of the Rio Serrano."

Maritza kept walking, leaving out the fact that they needed to reach the top of the river at the mountain's peak by midnight.

* * *

When they reached the base of the Sierra Nacer, the sun was well into the sky and the air was chilled. Maritza's thin jacket and hat wouldn't do too much for her up at the top, but it was better than nothing. She looked up the daunting slate, searching for a pathway. The mountain seemed to stretch all the way to the clouds now that she was just below it. *Just how small am I in the world?* she wondered. The only path she could make out was the one carved out by the thinning river. The rushing water was too dangerous. Seeing no other options, she grabbed onto a notch on the mountainside and started pulling herself up.

"You are crazy," said Fausto. His voice shook, but he was already doing the same.

Maritza's arms burned with her weight as she continued up the mountain. She winced every time she heard a tumbling pebble because if she missed a step, then that would be the end of everything.

Her fingers were getting numb from grasping the jagged stones in the cold air. Finally they reached a landing and not soon enough for a stream of wind blew against their backs and they hugged the landing waiting for it to pass.

When the wind quelled they pulled

themselves up and shook out their stiff hands. Maritza looked at the sun, stunned by how long it'd taken them to climb, and they weren't that high. They were high, but she could still see the ground clearly. Fausto was bent down looking at the landing.

"Did you find anything?" she asked.

"The edges here look like they are intentional. I think this is a path."

They eyed the length of the landing and sure enough further ahead it took a sharp turn twisting up the mountainside. The path was thin but Maritza could make out a zigzagging pattern chiseled right into the stone.

* * *

Maritza and Fausto made their way up the curving path, pressing their backs to the wall when the path was too thin. The wind was icy now and coming in more frequent bursts. Fausto was wrapped in her hat and Papá's *chamanto* in an attempt to keep warm. The wind whistled as it flowed over the sharp edges of the gray mountain. Maritza pulled the collar of her jacket over half of her face, thankful again for Fausto drying out their clothes.

They were nearly half way up the mountain and more exposed when Maritza saw the wall. The wall was flat and completely smooth. It ran the length of the narrow landing and cut off to a sheer drop. Fausto shrugged his shoulders ready to move forward. He was freezing.

"Wait!" she called. "Someone put this here for a reason. Help me."

Fausto returned and grabbed Maritza's belt loop as she leaned over the mountain edge to examine the wall. And that is all it was. Maritza found the wall was only a few inches thick and was truly an opening to...

"The temple," she whispered.

Fausto pulled her back to the landing. His brows were furrowed and his teeth chattered.

"Did...you see...anything?" he asked.

"I found the temple, we'll get you warm soon," Maritza answered.

She pressed against the edge of the wall and reached her foot across it until she found the opposing ledge. She swung herself to the other side and peeked around motioning for Fausto to do the same.

When they were safe inside the temple opening, Maritza looked at the engraving marking the entrance. There were spots and tails cut into the smooth walls. *Jaguars, good.* Maritza ran her fingers over the graceful carvings. The corridor quickly faded to black. Maritza dug out Abuela's candle and matches. Many of the matches had been damaged beyond use during the river crossing, but she finally struck one and lit the candle.

The temple was much larger than its outward appearance suggested. The carved walls dwarfed Maritza and Fausto. Dust floated around them like flies and the air was so stuffy and stale that Maritza yearned for the river water. As they continued down the halls, they saw pictures drawn along the walls. The fading paints of burnt orange and white told stories of the Incas bringing sacrifices to Roca in hopes of receiving rain for the crops, favorable fertility, and healthy, strong warriors.

Maritza and Fausto came across a row of

wooden torches and lit one for each of them. The candle light had not been enough. Very soon they were grateful to have found the torches. Not only were they considerably warmer but they'd come to an obstacle. Before them, the ground cut off. Instead, in the blackness, there was a circular stone pillar. The flat top didn't hold anything and was just far enough that they couldn't walk to it. Beyond the pillar was more darkness, the torch light could not reach to the far recesses. Fausto kicked a broken stone off of the edge and listened for the rock to hit the bottom, but they heard nothing. Maritza had already made up her mind and was hopping to the pillar. Fausto stayed quiet long enough for her to balance herself.

"You are going to give me a heart attack!" his voice echoed. "What are you doing?"

"You're too young for a heart attack," said Maritza, not looking back at him.

"Not really," he said under his breath.

"Besides," she continued, "there isn't any other way. I can see another pillar in front of me. They must lead all the way back. It's only big enough for one person so wait for me to get to the next one."

Maritza hopped to the next pillar, then the next. The darkness surrounded her. She wasn't afraid, but she didn't want the pillars to go on forever and she still couldn't see an end in sight. She was six stones in before she realized that Fausto wasn't behind her. She tiptoed around and was relieved to see his torch still floating in the air, but he hadn't jumped to the first pillar.

"Fausto, what's wrong?" she called back.

"I cannot go this way," he said. "I do not like heights. Last time I was trapped for years in the darkness. If we fall here, I do not think we will survive."

"But we've come so far. Here I'll come back and help you. Or if you want, you can wait here for me."

"We should not separate. One of us might get hurt."

"Then you have to come with me because I'm not turning back now."

Maritza watched as Fausto's flame fidgeted from side to side, and then closer. *He's moving,* she thought as she heard his shoes slap onto the stone. Soon he'd crossed four pillars but he stopped moving. He was close enough to see now and what Maritza saw made her worried. He was frozen still, his teeth clenched and his eyes shut tight. *He's afraid. What can I do to help him?*

"Look Fausto," she said trying to grab his attention. "Watch me, it's easy. Just like swimming."

This was not like swimming but she was trying to give him confidence. She turned back and jumped to another pillar. One, two, three. On the third she looked ahead, *Another clearing, this is the last one.* It was a bit further than the rest and she had to push hard to make the jump. She scooted back on the pillar and gave herself a single pace running start. She leapt, flying through the air and scraping her knee as her hands slammed onto the surface. She quickly picked up her torch hoping Fausto had kept his eyes closed just a little longer. *Now for him. He only needs to jump six more times.*

"Fausto, look I made it across! It's not far,"

she said. "Answer if you can hear me."

"I am here," he said. He sounded small.

"We're going to play a game. You like games, it'll be fun."

"I do not wish to play a game."

"This one is really fun. The girls in my village play it. I'm gonna sing a song and you jump when I spell your name. Okay?"

"I do not think so."

"Here I go! School school the golden rule. Pencil, paper, sign your name F-"

Fausto's torch didn't move. *This isn't going to work. He's afraid like I was at the river. But I had him there holding my hand. I can't do that for him here.*

"Fausto listen, you have to do this. You want to see your family right? Remember the first night under the tree? You told me that you weren't ready to give up. You kept on for years in the well. Don't quit now. We're almost there. Six more little hops you can do it!"

He stayed quiet for a while. His flame crackled, moving up and down with his breath.

"Can you sing it again?" he finally said.

"Of course," Maritza clutched her own

blazing torch. "School, school, the golden rule. Pencil, paper, sign your name

F-" the flame drew closer.

One, good he's moving.

"A-" closer still.

Two.

"U-"

Three, keep going. The walls shook violently around them, so hard Maritza had to plant her own feet to keep her balance. She knew Fausto must've been rattled, but she continue on. It was even more important for him to make it across.

"S-" she said through a cough from the surrounding dust.

Four, he's shaking again.

"You're doing so good Fausto only two more! T-"

Five, I can see him now!

"O!"

But Fausto didn't jump. He was looking at the gap separating him from the ledge. Maritza felt slightly guilty that she hadn't told him about it. She waved at him to put his attention back onto her.

"Fausto I'm here!" she cheered. "This is the last one and we're on our way! Just give yourself an extra push on this one. It's not far I made it."

Fausto nodded his head in agreement and took a step back.

"O!" Maritza yelled and as she did Fausto took the jump and let out a roar fit for a warrior. She was right there when he landed, grabbing his arm and pulling him away from the ledge.

"I think that makes us even," she said as she patted him on the shoulder.

Thank you Paula. She said to herself, not letting Fausto see just how worried she really was.

Chapter Twelve

This part of the temple was even more expansive than the other. Maritza couldn't see the ceiling, but she did make out more paintings. She imagined the portraits of mothers raising their babies over the river must have traveled to the very top. There was another torch, which Maritza lit so they could keep their bearings. On the opposite wall, scores of men with painted chests wore masks depicting war faces. Some masks bared sharp teeth while others stuck out wiggling tongues. Fausto lit a torch and started mimicking as many of the masks as he could. *I guess he's feeling better,* Maritza figured as she continued her search, staying close to the wall.

As she plunged deeper into the darkness, she kept her eyes trained on the floor. She didn't want any more surprises. However, instead of a cliff, she stepped on a golden coin. The reflection of the flames danced on the crudely printed face of the coin. Maritza picked it up weighing it in her hand. It was heavier than she expected. Maritza bit her lip and pressed forward. She'd barely taken three steps before the treasure was in sight. All along the wall lay piles of golden coins. Maritza spotted sparkling diamonds, sapphires, and pearls, anything one could dream of. Statues of women wearing thin robes lined the wall. The women held bowls atop their heads that held even more precious items. Even the eyes of the statues had gems in place of irises. Maritza had certainly never seen so many beautiful, valuable things. She was shaken out of her daydream when Fausto ran past her and swiped up a diamond tipped scepter. It was taller than he was with foreign engravings down the golden shaft.

"Aha!" he cried. "I am Fausto. King of the Andes!"

Torches lining the entire room blazed up simultaneously at Fausto's farce. The room was fully lit and Maritza could now see that treasures, statues and overloaded chests lined the entirety of the room. At the head of the enclosure was a painted carving of a large man sitting on a golden throne.

That must be Roca, Maritza gasped at the remarkable image. His beady eyes stared right at Maritza and his black hair spilled over the throne and onto the descending steps before him. At his feet people bowed to him, and above him was a stone carving of a jaguar designed as though it were pouncing forward. Maritza slapped the scepter from Fausto's hand. He opened his mouth to protest but she was already pointing at something else. In the center of the room was a thin, raised column.

In contrast to the decadence of the rest of the room, the column was quite plain. It was painted completely in white and the only decorations were elegantly curved edges and engravings of palm leaves. However, it was what the column housed that interested Maritza. Centered atop the column, in a deep black bowl, was the clear, crystal salt.

Maritza ran up to the bowl with Fausto right at her heels.

"Well?" Fausto said when Maritza didn't move. "Take it."

"I don't know how much," Maritza said. "Abuela didn't tell me."

"Just take all of it."

"We can't take it all. Right?"

"Why not? What does it matter? It is better to have too much, than not enough."

"But, what if someone else needs it?" *There were so much of the other items, but not this time*, she thought.

"What if someone else needs it? *Ay dios mio!* You have to be home tomorrow!"

Maritza didn't want to be greedy. Of course she wanted to grab the bowl and run home.

She'd come so far for this bit of salt. There probably weren't many people who found themselves in her situation, but if they did and they got here and there was no more salt, then what? As Maritza turned these thoughts over and over in her head, she heard a deep rumble. She turned in every direction trying to pinpoint a source, but it sounded as though it were everywhere.

The jaguar above the throned man peeled forward from the glimmering wall, leaving cracks where it was nestled. The jaguar landed with a thud that shook Maritza where she stood. She and Fausto retreated towards a wall and Fausto picked up the spear-like scepter, ready to defend. There was nowhere to run as the growls echoed throughout the hall.

"Children shouldn't play here," said the jaguar.

He grinned to show his sharpened fangs. His eyes were obsidian black and the outlines of his spots were carved into his body as smooth raised squares. The cat growled and his rocky shoulders protruded forward as he sauntered towards Fausto and Maritza. She knew they had to get out of there, but she didn't see an exit. All she could do was bide her time.

"Did you mean to take something of mine?" he continued. He looked at the scepter in Fausto's hand with a glare. "Greed can get you in trouble."

Fausto dropped the scepter and he and Maritza scooted about the beast back towards the column. The jaguar watched the scepter hit the floor before diving into the pile of treasure. He rolled around basking in the luxury. When he sat up, golden coins and gems slid from his stone body.

"I was greedy once. Hundreds of years ago The Creator sent me to this land. I helped the people in matters of war, harvest and health. Whatever they needed to prosper. I brought them knowledge and technology. It was not long before they began to worship me. They gave me the name Roca for my generous nature, and they were generous in return. I was only doing as I was told, but I reaped many

benefits.

I called them Mapuche, the people of the land. In the beginning they brought me small offerings. Animal pelts, fruits, and flowers. As days turned to months, and months to years the Mapuche learned many things. They mined gold and became fierce warriors. Whenever explorers tried to claim this land, the Mapuche swiftly tore them down and brought me the spoils to show their gratitude. Even this scepter was taken from a defeated fleet.

Before I knew it, they were making sacrifices to me and adorning me with exotic jewels. They even built this temple in my name, and called this very mountain 'Roca'. Glory was all to me!

It must have been a thousand years before the Mapuche started having their own ideas, expanding their knowledge and forgetting about me. But I was the one who'd given them everything. Without me they would be still stumbling about the forests. I made them!

They were no longer paying me tribute

and that would not do. One night, I decided to show them what happened when they forsook me. I left the temple and went to the villages. I burned their fields, spread sickness, I even stopped the river's flow. Panic spread throughout the land. 'The gods are angry!' they cried and once again offerings were brought in my name. The power of the people bowing before me and laying gold at my feet surged through me. But, it wasn't enough. Soon there was less and less gold. I demanded more but they insisted there wasn't any. One ridiculous woman even brought me that bowl of salt and begged me to heal her child.

I knew the Mapuche were lying and I went to find out what treasures they hid from me. On the darkest night, I crept into the hut of the Elder. He and his family slept, they hadn't even noticed my presence. Right in the center of the hut laid a succulent red ruby. It shimmered brilliantly even in the darkness. I knew they were liars. I snatched up my prize and swallowed it so that they would never hide it from me again.

But it was a trick! For when I had swallowed the gem, black smoke rose from the ground wrapping around me, suffocating me. When I awoke I was back in my temple. I felt heavy and when I looked down I saw that my once strong arms and legs were now stone paws.

'Roca,' came a voice. And I knew The Creator had returned.

'Father,' I answered, 'Set me free. I've done so much good!'

'You have been selfish. You were to help these people. Instead you are consumed with greed. You are no longer needed.'

'Father? Father? Father!'

I screamed until I was coarse, but he had gone. He'd trapped me in this wretched vessel and destroyed the path to the temple, leaving me alone amongst my treasures."

Maritza still hadn't thought of a plan by the time Roca finished his story. The only way would be through him. She wouldn't be able to snatch the salt and get herself and Fausto back across the pillars before he was on top of them. *What to do?* she thought squeezing Fausto's hand and wondering just when it was that she grabbed him.

"You remind me of the woman who brought the salt," Roca said to Maritza. "You have the same look of weary desperation in your eyes. What brought you here? Who are you trying to save?"

"My sister," said Maritza hiding the tremble in her voice, "Isidora. She's sick." She figured she shouldn't tell the greedy beast that Isidora was turning to gold.

"Your journey was in vain. I cannot leave here to heal her."

"Actually, I came for the salt. I was told if I came up the Sierra Nacer, I'd find your temple and the salt would be here. If I could have some of it we'll leave and we won't bother you again."

"Sierra Nacer?"

Roca's ears perked up and he leapt from the mound of gold. He circled about Maritza and Fausto, dragging his cold, stony tail beneath her chin.

"So," Roca purred. "They renamed *my* mountain? Whatever should I do? Maybe force my way out and make your people pay?"

"We do not want trouble," said Fausto, but Roca jumped and growled inches away from Fausto's face.

"I was not speaking to you boy," he said. Turning to Maritza he asked "And you girl. I've been alone many years, and the first person I see thinks she can take what is mine? Why do you want this salt?"

"I just need it," she said with her fists balled.

"You just...need it..."

Maritza shook her head in agreement. Roca stalked about the great hall eyeing the girl. His heavy paws thundered against the ancient floors with each step.

"Fine, the salt means nothing to me," he said. Maritza shoulders sagged with relief. "But, you must leave something in return."

"I don't have much to spare," she said.

She opened the sack and pulled out Abuela's candle and the fish that Fausto had caught.

"This is all I have," she pleaded.

"No, that will not do," replied the jaguar. "You have something much more valuable."

"There is nothing," Maritza said. But she knew there was. *I can't give him my last piece of Mamá.* Her hand shot to her necklace, covering the ring.

"It has been a long time since I have been brought tribute. That ring will do nicely," he said with a purr.

Maritza made a dash for salt, but Roca was too quick and his giant paw knocked her aside. Maritza slammed, coughing, onto the cold floor. Tears rippled in her eyes as the crackling flames flickered against the stones. She clutched onto the small ring and ran her fingertip across the imprinted rose.

"Don't cry girl," cooed Roca, "it is the way of the world. Sometimes a sacrifice must be made."

"But this is nothing, you have all of that gold this isn't even valuable."

"Yes, I can tell that it is low quality. However, you value it, so I value it."

Papá gave Mamá this ring. She wore it. We

don't have anything else of hers. How can I just let it go? Maritza was distraught.

"The choice is yours. You can give me the ring, or this Isidora can perish."

"You're cruel," she spat as she slipped the ring from her neck.

"Present it to me properly," the beast said. "Get on your knees and give it with both hands. Give me the feeling I have craved all these years."

Maritza sat up on her knees and held the ring in the palms of her hands. As she bowed her head she realized how bare she felt. She almost never removed the ring. She wanted to be selfish, but she knew she couldn't. Isidora's life was at stake. The tears she'd managed to hold in could not be contained. They splashed like raindrops onto the stone as Roca's sandpaper tongue licked the ring from her hands.

When Roca was satisfied he moved aside, clearing the path to the column. Maritza rose still sobbing and grabbed a handful of salt from the bowl. Fausto held the sack out for her. The painting of Roca in his human form rumbled as it slid to the side, revealing a passage with a light at the end.

"This will lead you back to the mountain path," Roca said. "Good luck girl."

Maritza gave the stony beast one last glare at his spiteful words, knowing he wasn't truly concerned for her or Isidora. Fausto put his arm around Maritza's shoulder and led her to the passage. She shuddered and wept, clutching the empty necklace. The green knot fell free, and the quipu had only one knot remaining.

Chapter Thirteen

When they broke free of the temple Maritza wiped her straggling tears. The moon had risen and she didn't have much time to find the final ingredient, the *rosa de palacio*. She stormed ahead up the chiseled path and climbed further up the mountain. They were on the back end and needed to circle around to the river. She was soon ahead of Fausto and he gave her the space. *I'm sorry Mamá,* she thought, *I didn't want to give up your beautiful ring. He gave me no choice.*

The air was colder now that night had come. Near the mountain's peak, Maritza was thankful the wind had ceased. Stars twinkled, larger than life, across the sky as the sliver of moon crept slowly to its highest point. When she looked up she could see snow capping the mountain peak. *There will be so much more in the coming months.*

The path finally curved around the mountain, but was so worn out by erosion that Maritza and Fausto had to inch their way around on their tiptoes. Maritza noticed Fausto was anxious. His fingers trembled and he avoided looking down, but he didn't speak up about it. They pressed their cheeks to the chilly mountainside, inching their way around. Maritza was first to reach the other side. As Fausto neared the edge there was a crackle, and as soon as he made it to Maritza a chunk of the path broke off, slid down and shattered against another landing. Maritza did her best to ignore the crumbling rocks toppling downward.

Maritza spotted the river. It wasn't more

than a couple feet wide. The foothills below seemed so far away. Above, the moon had nearly reached its goal. Maritza noticed a fog clouding only the other side of the river and hopped across the trickling water. The fog overtook her and when she looked back she could no longer see Fausto.

"Fausto?" she called.

"I am here. Where did you go?" he answered.

"Maritza," came a wafting voice.

Maritza spun around, but she didn't see anything. The fog was too thick.

"Who's there?" she asked.

"Where are you?" called Fausto.

"I'm in the fog," she said. "Don't come over yet."

"Zita come," came the voice again. It was soft and kind.

Maritza stumbled through the fog holding out her hands in front on her. *Who is calling me? Only Fausto calls me Zita. Only Fausto and...*

"Mamá?" Maritza called out. "Mamá is that you?"

"Zita" was all the voice said over and over.

Maritza continued blindly through the fog until she pushed a stone with her foot and heard it fall down a slope. She dropped to her knees and crawled along the ground feeling for any changes. *A cliff,* she thought when she found the dropping edge. She'd nearly walked off of it.

"Maritza," called Fausto. "Are you okay?"

"I'm fine. Just wait," She said.

"Zita," the voice emanated from the abyss. "What you seek is with me."

"Mamá, is that you?" Maritza asked again as she stared into the dense fog.

"Zita, have faith."

Have faith? Maritza thought. She couldn't see anything. Was the *rosa de palacio* even up here? *Faith is what will push us on,* she recalled Abuela's words. *This is completely insane.*

"Fausto! Wait for me until morning. If I'm not back when the sun rises, take everything to my Abuela in Santa Alma."

"What do you mean?" he asked.

She didn't have time to explain. The moon

was high. It would be midnight any moment. *Have faith Zita,* she told herself and dove from the cliff.

* * *

Wind slapped against Maritza's face as she hurdled through the swirling fog. Her long brown hair flicked in sharp patterns as she fell deeper and deeper. The flaps of her windbreaker made crinkling noises. Her screams were stifled by the pressure against her chest. Beaded tears were ripped from her watering eyes.

Darkness was approaching. Whatever she was about to hit was coming and coming fast. Maritza fought against the pressure forcing her arms in front of her face and waiting for the impact. She couldn't bear to watch. She closed her eyes when the marbled gray earth was close enough to see. But instead of hitting the surface, inches above the ground she came to an abrupt halt. Maritza opened her eyes as her hair cascaded over her, caressing the smooth stone.

Maritza released the breath that she hadn't realized she was holding. As she let out the little puff she floated to the ground. She looked up from where she came but all she saw was the swirling fog. Around her was nothing but grayness. Gray stone rose up and into the clouds. No way up unless you could sprout wings. To her left was a deep and dark trench. The borders were misshapen and bulbous. *That might be the way out,* she thought before looking to her right.

A jagged line split into the earth causing Maritza to pull back her feet in fear it would open up and swallow her whole. Her eyes widened, she sucked in her lower lip as she looked on in wonder. A green bulb popped out of the crack. As it grew, a twisted stem formed beneath it. The dense fog split, raining down a trail of moonlight. The beam traveled down the cavern and when it reached the growing plant, the bulb burst open. Burgundy silken petals curled outward and glistening pollen lingered just above. A warm, sweet perfume drifted from the rose and mixed with the chilled mountain air.

The rosa de palacio, Maritza thought. *Finally it's here.* She reached out her hand gingerly, remembering how Abuela had told her to be careful with it. She closed in on the beautiful bloom barely containing the tremble in her fingertips.

The chirping began low like a hum. Maritza hardly noticed it. The sharp sound grew intensely, and she wondered if she'd been tricked into trapping herself with no way to escape. Maritza pulled away from the rose, and searched for the source.

La Mujer Mojada. There can't be any crickets down here. This is...nowhere. Her eyes stopped, fixed on the deep dark cavern not a stone's throw away from her. The screeching song grew to a roar, bouncing between the hazy walls. Maritza steadied her breath, and waited for the Wet Woman to attack. But, nearly as quickly as it began, the chirping stopped.

"Zita," Maritza heard from the trench.

Maritza squared and blocked the sight of the rose. From the cleft a figure appeared. The frame was slender beneath a black flouncing dress that slid across the floor. It moved with quick elegant steps, almost as though it were gliding. When the figure came out of the shadows Maritza saw could tell it was a woman. Her hair was long and dark like the moonless sky. Loose curls fluttered around her shoulders as she continued forward. Her lips were tinted a translucent peach, and formed a warm smile. The woman was upon her when Maritza noticed her eyes. She would know them anywhere. Altogether she was warmed and horrified. Those light brown honey eyes belonged to Mamá.

Maritza backed further away careful not to crush the flower. She looked around hoping to find a weapon of any sort. Her own mother was La Mujer Mojada. A child snatcher. *No, Mamá would never. It's a trick*. Mamá must have seen the distress in Maritza's face, because sorrow crept into her eyes, and her smile wilted. Even though she was frightened and suspicious, Maritza felt dejected for hurting her mother's feelings, if it was her mother.

"I'm sorry," she said, but not moving closer. "Who are you?"

"Zita, it is me. Mamá."

"My Mamá died. A long time ago."

"I did Zita," she said stepping forward. "I came back to help you."

"Don't come any closer! You're evil. I heard the crickets. You take children away!"

"No dear. I don't. When I come to the children, they've already passed. I just, help them on their next journey. I was trying to make contact with you, but I couldn't."

"How do I know you're real?" Maritza had made her way to a wall.

"You had enough faith to follow me down here when I called. Is that not enough?"

Maritza held her stare, but stayed where she was.

"Don't you remember me?" the woman continued. "You and I used to go to the white fountain in the city. We would eat ham sandwiches and toss breadcrumbs to the birds. And sometimes I would make you close your eyes and when you'd open them I'd have a big cone of cotton candy for you. But only blue because you didn't like pink. Do you remember that?"

Of course Maritza remembered the fountain. It was one of her few cherished memories of Mamá. The fountain had been made of rounded white stone with four tiers. Bellflowers crowned the top tier and water flowed from them cascading over the lower tiers of crafted cherubs and ribbons. Maritza had gone back there as many times as she could, but it was never as grand as it was in her memory. Maritza wanted nothing more than for this woman to be her mother.
    "I remember," she said slowly.
    "And do you remember when I passed?" the woman said. "Isidora had just come into the world. I knew I wouldn't make it through the night. I called you over and squeezed your tiny hands. I gave you the ring Papá had given me when he asked me to marry him. You were too young to lose a mother and I'm so sorry that I had to leave you my little Zita."
    This was the memory Maritza tried to block out. Back then Mamá was so tired. Her lips were dry and sweat ran down the sides of her beautiful face. Maritza had dabbed her forehead with a wet cloth, but Mamá was so

hot. *I couldn't help her. Mamá was in pain and I couldn't do anything.*

When Mamá had given her the ring, Maritza stared into her eyes, there were dark circles beneath them. Mamá pulled her in for a kiss and slipped away. Even though she was gone, she was still lovely and looked to have simply fallen asleep. Maritza had pounded her tiny fists on Mamá's unmoving chest. She begged her to wake but even though she shouted and cried, it was not until Maritza was older, that she truly felt the loss and Roca had reopened the wounds she'd tried to heal.

Maritza often watched the other girls around the village with their mothers. She'd pretend she was one of them. She'd imagine the feeling of one of the mothers braiding her hair, or taking her to pick out a bottle of nail polish. She often wondered if Isidora felt the same, but could never ask her. Her sister's smiles were too sweet and Maritza never wanted her to know what it felt like to miss what she couldn't have. At times Maritza even felt angry at Mamá for leaving, but Mamá had come back for her now when she really needed her. This was her mother and Maritza ran into her open arms.

"Mamá!" she cried. "I lost your ring. I'm so sorry. A jaguar ate it."

"Don't cry my baby," Mamá said as she stroked Maritza's hair. "It's just a thing. You, Papá, and Isidora are my greatest treasure."

"Isidora is turning to gold. I didn't protect her. I saw the Alicanto but I didn't reach her in time."

"There was nothing you could do. I have been watching. Isi has an adventurous nature. But, you came here to save her like a good big sister. Don't be too angry with the Alicanto, he doesn't belong in this world. I will take him back with me."

Maritza looked up at Mamá and in the sky the Alicanto was flying in circles. His feathers had regrown and his golden wings rivaled the sun. He swooped down into the cavern and curled himself in a corner. Maritza didn't see any of the frantic anger in his glowing eyes he'd had in the cave. He only looked free as he bowed his head to her.

"He is thankful to you for waking him," said

Mamá.

"I thought he wanted to eat us," Maritza said with a small laugh.

"He won't be bothersome anymore," Mamá smiled. "Now for you Zita. You've done so well coming all this way. I'm so proud, but you have to get back home."

"Do you know what's happening there? Is everyone okay?" Maritza asked as she looked towards the *rosa de palacio*.

"I have been checking in. Papá is as handsome as ever, and Isidora is growing so beautifully. You both are. Everything is fine for now but you must hurry."

Maritza walked to the rose with Mamá's hand at her back. She looked up at Mamá and waited for her nod before she picked the flower. The stem was fuzzy and when Maritza pulled it from the ground she was surprised by how light it was for such a grand flower.

"Zita, it's time for me to go."

"Not yet," Maritza said she snapped her head around. "Why couldn't you come to me before? I needed you."

"The bread."

"The bread? What bread?"

"That little slice of bread you stuffed in your pocket. Homemade bread, made by Abuela who loves you very much. You were too tethered the world of the living. It wasn't until you lost it in the river that I could even get close. But, it's alright. You never needed me."

"I'll always need you Mamá."

"And you'll always have me. This is all I can do for now. Your journey is not over, but mine is my dear. You went through so much, but you have to get back to Isidora now. The new moon is tomorrow night."

"We have time, let me stay," she pleaded.

"Ah, I know this," Mamá said as she spotted the quipu. "Abuela told me about the quipu."

"She gave it to me before I left. She said it would help me all the way, but I don't know how."

"She was right to give it to you. You only have one knot left. Let's see here."

Mamá ran her hand across the rope lying on Maritza's neck. The reds, yellows, and purples seemed to glow beneath her touch. When she reached the purple knot, it fell open in her palm.

"Just as I thought," she said. "Your faith was the last step to your true self. You've been reborn new. But, this rope didn't make you a different person, it just showed you what was always inside. You made a friend, solved a riddle, you were brave, gave up something precious to you, and now you've taken a leap of faith."

Maritza stared up into Mamá's eyes speechless as the quipu was laid onto her neck. She drew her fingers across the smoothed quipu. She'd barely noticed the unraveling knots. *What was always inside?*

"Take all the lessons you've learned on your journey and teach Isidora. Tell her and Papá that I love them and thank Fausto for me. He took care of my girls."

"Mamá, I love you," Maritza said as she pressed her face into Mamá's bosom.

"I love you too Zita. And remember, I will always be looking down on you."

Mamá pressed a kiss to Maritza's forehead and backed away. The Alicanto scooped Mamá onto his neck and the two flew into the darkness of the trench. Mamá's shadow was just out of sight when the fog coiled around Maritza and the rose she'd come for.

Chapter Fourteen

The fog dispersed from around her and Maritza was back atop the Sierra Nacer, *rosa de palacio* in hand. Fausto was there. He'd crossed the river and now was snoozing on the ledge. Maritza could see the first rays of morning peeking over the mountaintop. Mamá had said she was born anew, and Maritza felt new. She was ready to go home. She knelt down and tapped Fausto on his nose.

"I am awake!" he shouted with a start. He saw Maritza and relief washed over his face. "Where were you? After you told me to wait I crossed over, but the fog was gone. I called for you all night."

"Mamá says 'thank you'," she said as she held up the rose to him.

"So it's time to go home," he said.

"Yeah let's go!" but Fausto didn't look as excited as she'd expected.

Maritza gently laid the *rosa de palacio* in the sack and took it from Fausto, he'd carried it since they crossed the river. He'd done so much. As they made their way down the mountain Maritza told him all about Mamá and what she'd said.

"Did you see the Alicanto?" she asked.

"No I did not. You are making it up," he joked, but his smile didn't reach his eyes.

"No I'm not! Maybe I should call him to eat you up!"

They were nearing the bottom when their path was cut short. Broken shards of rock blocked the path and it was too far to jump the rest of the way down. *There must've been a landslide,* Maritza thought. She approached the block and started throwing off the smaller rocks. Fausto joined her and they worked for a long time in silence. After some time she noticed Fausto had lost his energy and was doing little more than kicking at the smaller stones.

"Let's take a break," she said, though she really didn't want to. She could see the sun rising higher in the sky, and they had a long ways to go.

"Good idea," Fausto said as he sat against a wall and sighed.

"Do you want a piece of fish?" she asked.

"No thank you. It has probably turned bad anyway."

"Well it might be okay. Did I ever tell you about the time I caught a giant tuna with my bare hands?"

Fausto gave a polite smile in response, but Maritza easily saw he wasn't very interested in her made up story. He was the funny one after all. Even so, Maritza wished she knew how to help her friend.

"I bet Princess Young would like to hear about your Mamá," he said after a while. "We should stop by and tell her."

"Fausto," Maritza said carefully, "you know we can't. The new moon is tonight and we have to hurry."

"Yeah I know," he nodded his head.

"What's really wrong?" she asked as she closed her hand over his. "You can tell me."

"I...I just want the adventure to keep going."

"It has been pretty fun I guess, but only because you're here. You know Isi is waiting."

Fausto didn't say anything. He sat there flicking pebbles from the ledge. Maritza didn't know what to say and decided to keep quiet as well. And then it dawned on her. *How could I have been so thoughtless?* she realized. *I am going home to Papá, Abuela, and Isi, but Fausto still doesn't know if his family will be there when we get back.* Maritza felt ashamed she hadn't thought much of what would happen to her friend, but she wanted to make it up to him. She took the quipu from around her neck and put it around his. He looked up at her and raised his eyebrows with a silent question.

"Mamá looked at the quipu and pulled the final knot from it. She said my faith helped me in my last step. Now you have to have faith in yours. I don't know if we'll find your family, but you can trust that even if we don't, you will still be a part of my family. Besides, Papá will want to meet the 'King of the Andes' that helped save his daughters. With you by my side, I'm sure the adventure will never end."

Fausto squeezed the quipu and his face lit up. He gave Maritza his big charming smile and stood up. He pressed his palms to the last boulder. Maritza joined him and they gave one final push. The boulder toppled down to the foothills. Before they knew it, they were down the path and sliding the rest of the way to the fields. With the Sierra Nacer at their backs, they were on their way home.

* * *

They'd run all day and into the evening taking as few breaks as possible to make up for the hours spent on the mountain. Nonetheless, by the time they were outside of Mijas night had fallen. The pristine greeting sign was only yards away. Maritza looked to Fausto to see how he was feeling. Determination was written across his face and he was the first to step forward.

When they entered the village, only a few people were around the square. Fausto spun around as he searched every direction. Maritza could tell that he didn't recognize much of his home. It had been years since he'd been back.

"Do you see anyone you know?" she asked.

"I'm not sure," he answered. She could hear the frustration in his voice.

"Where is your house?"

"I think it was that way," he said pointing "but there are so many new buildings."

"Maybe we should ask someone?"

"If I could just..." he spun, looking for anyone, anything familiar.

"Listen Fausto," Maritza said eyeing the rising moon, "I don't have much time. I still have to get home. Come home with me and we'll look tomorrow. I promise."

"Just a few more minutes," he said before darting towards his old home.

"Fausto!" Maritza called and behind her someone dropped a clay pot.

Maritza turned around at the sound, it'd stopped Fausto in his tracks. Amidst the shattered, pieces stood a middle-aged woman. Her hair was pulled into a tight ponytail and Maritza could see streaks of gray in the thin starlight. She wore tan sandals and a white cotton dress. She was looking past Maritza at Fausto, and he saw her as well.

"Fausto?" she said. Her voice sounded strained, like she'd been yelling for a long time.

Fausto had been walking back to the center of the village when he heard his name. His eyes widened with recognition and he burst into a sprint. He ran into the arms of the mysterious woman.

"Anita!" his words were muffled as he held her tight.

Maritza smiled glad that Fausto had found someone and turned to head to Santa Alma. She'd waited too long there were only a few hours until midnight.

"Zita!" Fausto said. Maritza didn't want to stop, but she did. "This is my little sister Anita."

"Thank you, thank you." Anita said before Maritza could utter a word. "We thought he was lost to us forever. Our parents will want to meet you. Please, come."

"You're welcome, but Fausto helped me much more than I helped him. I'd love to meet them but I can't stay. I have to go now," Maritza said and turned once again to leave.

"Wait," Fausto said as he grabbed her. "Thank you again."

"I should be the one thanking you," Maritza said.

"No really. I was afraid to come home but you believed, so I believed. Tomorrow I will come visit you and meet your sister. I promise."

Fausto grabbed Maritza's shoulders, pulled her in and laid a kiss on her cheek. Once more, Maritza felt her cheeks flush. Fausto returned to Anita and the two walked off towards what must've been their home. She gently touched her cheek before running up the hill to Santa Alma.

Chapter Fifteen

Maritza reached the border of her village. She was panting and her brow was lined with sweat but she was glad she'd made it. She ran through the dusty village center and turned down the alley towards her home. With her heart light, she petted a black cat that was lying on a window sill. She blew a kiss when he turned his green eyes on her. She really did feel like a new person. She'd only been gone a few days but home felt different to her. The dust smelled like moist soil ready for seeding. The buildings looked like a royal kingdom. Maritza had never loved Santa Alma more.

When she reached the yellow house she saw the flickering flames from the candles beneath the door. The gravity of the situation fell over her. What would Isidora look like? Would Papá be angry? Was Abuela right about the new moon? She'd come this far and had to go just a little further. She squeezed the straps of the satchel and pushed the door open.

Papá and Abuela were bent over Isidora. When he heard the door Papá rushed over and swept Maritza up in his arms and hugged her tight. After he let go she saw the whites of his eyes were strung with red streaks and she was regretful for having caused him pain.

"Mari," he said, "how could you go out there alone? You should have found me, it could've been dangerous."

"There wasn't time Papá," she answered. "Besides, a friend helped me and I got everything just like Abuela said."

"You made a friend?" Papá couldn't hide his surprise.

"Later later," Abuela called from Isidora's side.

Maritza braced herself to see Isidora. *There's still time,* she said to herself. Though she reminded herself over and over, when she passed Papá and looked down to Isidora, she wasn't so sure. Isidora was nearly covered in gold. The whole of her body shined against the fire. Even her hair lay in golden tresses. Only her face was uncovered but Maritza noticed the edges of her oval visage changing slowly but surely. Maritza went to her and grabbed her hand. Isidora was stiff and Conejito was wedged in the crook of her arm. Maritza wanted to scream for her to wake, but she knew Isidora couldn't hear her.

Abuela pulled Maritza up and away from Isidora. They had work to do. She put a copper pot on the table they shared. Maritza nodded and gathered the items she'd collected and placed them on the table: the water-filled canteen, the apple, rosemary, salt, and finally the wine red *rosa de palacio*. Abuela smiled at Maritza and brushed back her hair.

"I knew you could do it *mi nieta*," Abuela said. Pride was written on her face.

"Mamá was glad you sent me," Maritza confessed.

Abuela tilted her head in a thought before leading Maritza to the pot.

"Let's do this together," she said.

Maritza poured the well water into the pot as Abuela sliced the apples.

"Don't use the core!" Maritza said more loudly than she intended. She remembered what Princess Young said. "The seeds are poisonous."

Abuela hesitated, but decided to trust Maritza and cut away the core and the bad seeds. As Abuela diced the slices, juice ran onto from the firm flesh. She put the pot over the fire and gave Maritza a pestle and mortar. Maritza placed the rosemary into the stone bowl and ground up the herb. The scent of mint and pine filled the house as though they'd decorated a Christmas tree.

Papá looked out of the window and into the

night sky. When he faced Maritza she could tell he was worried. *We must be running out of time,* she thought. The water was boiling and Abuela scooped the apples into the steaming water and they disintegrated as soon as they hit the bottom of the pot. When Maritza added the crushed rosemary the steam spilled from the pot into flourishes across the floor. Abuela picked up a pinch of the salt and held it over the pot.

"Wait Abuela," Maritza said remembering sacrificing Mamá's ring. "Please let me do it."

"Just a pinch," Abuela said, "and then the rose."

Maritza took a pinch of the salt and looked at it between her fingers. She'd given up something so precious for such a small amount. She tossed it into the pot and the boil became more rapid. The sweet sticky bubbles burst before they could fully form.

Last was the *rosa de palacio*. Maritza held the rose by its stem, glad she hadn't damaged it on the way home. She brought it over the furious water and when she moved to drop it in the petals fell off instead. The dark petals swirled around the pot and the boiling ceased. The petals melted turning the liquid a deep crimson and when Abuela took the pot from the fire to hand to Maritza, it was cool to the touch.

"It's ready," said Abuela.

Maritza knelt beside Isidora with the concoction. In the time she and Abuela had taken to brew the mix, gold had crept over Isidora's eyes. The mask was beautiful but too deadly. Maritza put the pot to Isidora's still soft lips. *Please, please, please*, she wished as she poured every last drop of the elixir into her mouth.

The family sat around the sleeping girl. They held hands and bowed their heads. All they could do was wait. For a long while nothing changed. Minutes felt like hours. Isidora got no worse, but she was not better. Midnight was on the brink when Maritza couldn't take anymore. She regretted taking the little girl for granted and she regretted not being able to protect her. *This is all my fault. I should never have run away!* She clutched Isidora's hand. It was hard and stiff.

"Isi," she cried as she pressed her forehead to Isidora's. "It's time to wake up! Papá and Abuela miss you. I miss you. I'm sorry I was jealous that you could make friends. Wake up and forgive me. I'll do anything."

Papá tried to pull Maritza away, but she would not be soothed.

"I tried to save you," she continued. "I went on an adventure! I made a friend, Fausto, and I brought back all these special things for you. And I saw Mamá! She said you were beautiful. She loves you and wants you to live on."

"Mari," came Papá's shaky voice.

She looked at him still frantic, but he was pointing at Isidora. Maritza could barely see through the tears flooding her eyes. But when she wiped them, she saw the cracks trickling down the gold of Isidora's tiny frame. Sparkling fractures covered the little girl from head to toe. Once she was all covered the golden cast shattered. Chunks fell to the floor revealing Isidora's brown skin beneath. Maritza brushed the golden shards from Isidora. *It's working.* She shook Isidora trying to wake her.

"Isi? Isi?" she begged. But the girl did not wake. "I saw the Alicanto, did you ever see him? He was magnificent and gold. He didn't mean to hurt you and Mamá took him home with her. And do you know how important bread is? And! And remember your favorite story? The princess in the tree? Well I found the princess Isi. She's *really* a tree! I met her. Her name is Princess Young and she wants to meet you."

The night was silent. No one was moving outside, even the wind refused to blow. The candles had nearly burned out. The pounding of Maritza's heart was so loud in her ears, she thought it would explode.

"Princess Young?" came Isidora's quiet, dry voice.

Maritza froze, squeezing Isidora's softening hand. The house was quiet. No one could say a word. Maritza almost forgot to breath, but when she did the family wrapped tighter together.

"Yes!" Maritza said laughing through her tears. "Princess Young."

"What happened?" Isidora asked as her eyes

fluttered open. "Did I find the treasure?"

"Sort of," Maritza said picking up one of the golden pieces.

Papá picked the girls up in his arms and showered kisses on both of them. His girls were safe and sound.

* * *

It'd been two weeks and the moon was full. The village had once again gathered around the fire for a fantastic tale. Abuela chatted with some of the other blue haired women and Paula played hand games with her girlfriends. The little twins pretended to dance with finely dressed dolls. Fausto had come and was as bouncy as ever boasting about being able to jump clear over a tree if he really wanted to. Nestled beside him was Isidora. Her golden hair tousled around her head every time she laughed at his jokes. Her shining hair was the only clue left that anything had happened at all. Maritza and Papá stood in the center of the circle by the flickering flames. He draped his *chamanto* over her head and everyone applauded for her debut. Papá blew his jubilant tune into the pan flute and backed away, leaving all eyes on her. Maritza stepped into the light, standing taller than ever.

"Now for a new legend," she said full of strength. "The story of *La Niña Dorada*, the golden girl!"

Acknowledgments

Many many thanks to all of my friends and family who have supported my journey as a writer. Thank you to my parents who made me read as punishment instilling a great love of literature. Thank you Alexis for motivating me when I put my writing dreams on the back burner, and for being tough on me when I needed it.

Maritza's Quipu

Quipus were used as counting tools by the ancient peoples of the Andes. You can make one too!

You'll need a ball of yarn (use many colors to mimic the look of Maritza's quipu), scissors and a ruler.

1. Use the scissors to cut 3 lengths of rope, 16 inches each. Use the ruler to measure.
2. Tie a knot at one end. Braid the 3 lengths of rope together to make the necklace. Tie a knot at the other end.
3. Cut 5 lengths of rope using the different colored yarns, 6 inches each.
4. Tie the 5 lengths of rope to your necklace, spacing them out 2 inches apart.
5. Tie a knot in each of the 5 decorative lengths wherever you like.

Now your quipu is ready for your adventure!

Discussion Questions

1. Why does Maritza feel so guilty when Isidora becomes ill? What makes her think it is her fault?

2. Why does Maritza have trouble making friends? Do you understand her feelings? Why do you think she became friends with Fausto?

3. Why did Princess Young choose to remain a tree? What would you do in her position and why?

4. Maritza had to make sacrifices to save Isidora. What did she sacrifice? What made those sacrifices hard for her?

5. Think about what strength means to you. In what ways is Maritza strong?